"AN OUTRAGE TO
AMERICAN GIRLHOOD"

That's what critics called DAISY MILLER when
Henry James wrote it. Now it is considered a
classic, one of his finest short novels; and, certainly,
one of his most popular. This poignant drama of
fleeting youth and innocence and its tragic ruin is
recaptured in Peter Bogdanovich's new film.

D0716732

DAISY MILLER
CAST

Cybill Shepherd—Annie P. Miller

Barry Brown—Frederick Winterbourne

Cloris Leachman—Mrs. Ezra B. Miller

Mildred Natwick—Mrs. Costello

Eileen Brennan—Mrs. Walker

Duilio Del Prete—Mr. Giovanelli

James McMurtry—Randolph C. Miller

Nicholas Hones—Charles

George Morfogen—Eugenio

DAISY MILLER

by

HENRY JAMES

WARNER
PAPERBACK
LIBRARY

A Warner Communications Company

WARNER PAPERBACK LIBRARY EDITION
FIRST PRINTING: JUNE, 1974

An Interview with Peter Bogdanovich
COPYRIGHT © 1974 BY MARTIN RUBIN
ALL RIGHTS RESERVED.

PHOTOGRAPHS COP. GHT © 1974 BY PARAMOUNT PICTURES
CORPORATION. ALL RIGHTS RESERVED

WARNER PAPERBACK LIBRARY IS A DIVISION OF WARNER BOOKS, INC.,
75 ROCKEFELLER PLAZA, NEW YORK, N.Y. 10019.

 A Warner Communications Company

Printed in the United States of America

CONTENTS

AN INTERVIEW WITH PETER BOGDANOVICH

by

Martin Rubin

Peter Bogdanovich's film credits include TARGETS (1968; director-producer-writer), THE LAST PICTURE SHOW (1971; director-co-writer), the feature-length documentary, DIRECTED BY JOHN FORD (1971), WHAT'S UP DOC? (1972; director-producer-co-writer), and PAPER MOON (1973; director-producer). His sixth film, DAISY MILLER, was shot on the actual locations referred to in James's story; principal photography began August 20, 1973 in Rome and was completed November 8 in Vevey, Switzerland. Mr. Bogdanovich has also written several books on the movies, the latest being PIECES OF TIME, a 1973 ESQUIRE-ARBOR HOUSE publication. He contributes a monthly column on Hollywood to **New York Magazine.** The following interview took place at Mr. Bogdanovich's home in Bel Air, California, February 18-19, 1974.

How did you come across Daisy Miller?

Just one of those things I read. It's interesting, the way this has worked out, because I was going to do *The*

Apple Tree, a story written by John Galsworthy in 1916. Actually, the story is similar to *Daisy Miller* in many ways: it's a love story about missed opportunities, it's about class differences, it's about an unwillingness to commit oneself emotionally to something that is alien or different.

But Galsworthy's story is much more sentimental. The girl in it is completely different. She's a little like Rima in *Green Mansions,* an innocent savage. Her name is Megan, a Welsh girl in the hills of Devon. This Englishman up from Oxford falls in love with her one summer, and she with him. He goes to town to buy her some clothes so he can take her away, and he doesn't have the nerve to go back. Twenty-five years later he comes to the area again and remembers. At that point he finds out that after he left the girl committed suicide.

I had been planning to do this story since I was about sixteen. For years I tried to get the rights, but they eluded me. At one time, they were owned by Jesse Lasky's widow—Lasky had meant to make the picture in the '40s with John Mills and Elizabeth Taylor. Finally, when I went to Warner Brothers to make *What's Up, Doc?,* it turned out that Warner now owned the rights, and I was free to make it. So I hired Gavin Lambert to write the screenplay, and it was quite a good script, but I just didn't want to make it. Like many beloved projects, you want to do it for so long that by the time you do get to do it you just don't want to anymore. It's almost as though you'd made it already and so there's no longer any challenge left.

Then I was developing yet another story based on an incident that happened to an Italian friend of mine when he stayed at the Plaza Hotel in New York: he came out around two in the morning, it was so hot, and found an absolutely stunning girl lying on the fountain, asleep. In the story, she turns out to be this girl from Texas, a real Amazon, who hits him every time he makes a pass at her. Then it went into a cross-country trip—what I really wanted to do was to make *Lolita,* but it was not possible. I thought it would be funny with, say, Cybill Shepherd and Marcello Mastroianni. We tried to develop it, but it didn't work out, probably because it was just one good incident that wouldn't develop into a script.

So I didn't have a picture. Around about here, somehow or other, I read *Daisy Miller* again, not having read it for many years. And it seemed exactly the right thing to do, like a sign from heaven, because there was the whole idea of an Italian versus American background, which I had become interested in after going to Rome in 1969. And it also had the same basic idea as *The Apple Tree,* the same theme of missed opportunities, yet done better, much more elegantly and less sentimentally. And a great part for Cybill Shepherd, with whom I had wanted to make another picture ever since *The Last Picture Show.* So there we were.

What's most immediately striking about the film Daisy Miller *is how faithful it is to the book. This seems a very different problem from, say,* The Last Picture Show, *where you were more involved in adaptation: selecting and cutting it down. In this film, it's more a question of interpretation than adaptation. Why did you decide to stick to the original so closely?*

Actually, when I first decided to do the story I thought it wasn't enough for a movie. So originally Frederic Raphael and I developed a much longer story and took a lot of license with Henry James. The dialogue, for instance, was very different; it was almost all new. There were several additional incidents—such as Winterbourne sneaking up to Daisy's room and going through her things when she was out.

So that it became more like an obsession. . . .

Right, like Jimmy Stewart in *Vertigo* or Dana Andrews in *Laura.* He was sniffing around her stuff—it became sick in a rather obvious way. And then when Winterbourne saw her with Giovanelli at the Colosseum, he rode off on a horse to the seashore, where he went into a kind of fit—his money was stolen—and it became very Dostoyevskian. Everything was also made much more explicit in terms of Daisy; she became aggressive in what was not an 1878 manner. I'm afraid I collaborated in this somewhat, and I condoned it.

I really didn't get a chance to read the original story again until I was on my way over to Europe to make the picture. But when I did, I suddenly realized that the story had been lost, that what was delicate and subtle about it had been lost behind a kind of Russian-Jewish adaptation. And I started going through the story and saying, "My God, look at all this good dialogue that's not being used!" There was a lot to do in terms of making the dialogue just a little bit easier to say, but the *ideas* for the dialogue that James wrote were wonderful. The more I read the story, the more I saw that anything obviously overlaid on it would destroy it. It was a fragile tale, and if I was going to change it in any way, it had to be done in terms of interpretation rather than in the actual sequence of events.

But frankly it wasn't my main concern that the picture be faithful to Henry James. I didn't think, "I must be faithful to the story, or else Leon Edel and all the James scholars will be up in arms." If I had been able to think of something that was better than Henry James, in terms of telling the story, I would have done it. It's just that I thought his original stuff was better than what Raphael or I had invented. So where the movie does do something different, it's because I thought it was an improvement, or a way of fleshing out and interpreting the story or visualizing something that wasn't dealt with.

I think it's a terribly good story; however, I do feel that it is a sketch rather than a finished canvas. When James originally wrote *Daisy Miller,* he subtitled the story "A Study." Some people have wondered what he meant by that. I think perhaps James himself wondered what he meant by it, since he dropped the subtitle for the New York edition. I interpreted it this way: when a painter does a sketch for a larger canvas, he often calls that a study. In his later career James did much larger canvases—*A Portrait of a Lady,* for one—on the same theme.

So, to me, *Daisy Miller* was always a sketch. Now I'm not doing a short movie or a sketchy one. I'm doing a feature, and I can't afford to be sketchy. But for the same reason, I would prefer to do *Daisy Miller,* as opposed to *A Portrait of a Lady* or *What Maisie Knew,* because I've got somewhere to go with it. It seemed to me there were enough hidden ambiguities that could be given some fleshing out, simply by putting actors in the roles and interpreting it a certain way. When Orson Welles made *Othello,* he didn't care so much about literalizing Shakespeare as he did about visualizing a lot of the things that in the play were spoken. I didn't do at all the same thing, but I do hope that the movie of *Daisy Miller* can stand on its own, and won't be forever stapled to the book.

It would seem that your experience directing on the stage was more useful for this film than any of your others. You mentioned that your attitude in the film would have to come through mainly in interpretation rather than changing things, and this strikes me as somewhat like stage direction. For instance, one of the most important scenes, both in the book and the movie, occurs when Winterbourne talks to Daisy at Mrs. Walker's dinner party. There are three very important exchanges in that scene. In the first one, Winterbourne

tells Daisy, "Your habits are those of a ruthless flirt,"
and she says, "Of course I'm a flirt. Did you ever hear
of a nice girl that wasn't?" In the next one, Winter-
bourne says, "They don't understand that sort of thing
here," and Daisy replies, "I thought they understood
nothing else!" Then, at the end of the scene, he says,
"I've offered you excellent advice," to which Daisy
comes back with, "I prefer weak tea!" All three lines
are very important in the book, but in the movie the
second one is the least emphasized, while James makes
a big thing out of it, even adding a line about Daisy's
"startling world-knowledge." And this is what you're
doing throughout the film, picking what to emphasize
and what to underline.

I don't like to spell out anything for an audience. In
fact, that scene is done in the movie without a cut,
until Daisy stands up. I think it's terribly important,
particularly in this movie, to pay attention, because
there's a lot more going on than you think there is.
It's the cumulative effect of the scene that's important
to me, rather than each individual moment, because
otherwise you can start cutting in and emphasizing
every line. But it seems to me you just have to play it
like a scene and the way people are.

People never react in normal conversation. I may
say something that shocks the hell out of you, but you
wouldn't show it on your face at all. Now James says
that Winterbourne was struck by her world-knowledge.
But he doesn't say that Winterbourne's face reflected
that shock. I'm always surprised at how little people
react in life, in normal conversation. So it seemed to
me that if it was going to be an honest scene, you
didn't want to overemphasize anything. Let the audience discover the meaning of it.

It was important to me that the audience should
watch the scene, pay attention, and then at the *end* of
it, when Daisy says, "I prefer weak tea," and walks

away, you're left with Winterbourne's reaction to the *whole* scene. He's left watching her walk away—as he does through the whole picture—watches her walk away, until she doesn't come back again. And he watches her with this expression of "What? I don't understand what just happened." It isn't just the "weak tea" line he's reacting to—it's the whole scene, the point of which is that Daisy knows a lot more than you think she does.

There's another emphasis you use, when Winterbourne meets Daisy at Hadrian's Villa. (In the story, it's the Palace of the Caesars.) He says, "I do want to say something," then he hesitates—"I want to say that your mother tells me she believes you're engaged."

Yes, that moment is pretty much invented by me; it's really not exactly that way in the story. To me, the whole movie is right in that moment. It seems to me that if Winterbourne had said anything at that moment, it might have been all right, at least in terms of their relationship. And you can see that Daisy is terribly disappointed that he doesn't say anything. You see, he's just unable—that's why he's so pathetic, apart from being reprehensible. He's unable to come out and say it to her because of his jealousy, because of his repression. And then he's left perplexed, which is how that silly ass is left every time throughout the picture.

Then some people say to me, "Well, why was she like that?" or "Why didn't he just come out and tell her he loves her?" They don't understand the mystery that goes on there, that terrible repression. And they don't understand *her* any more than Winterbourne did, which only proves that the story's still timely.

Although Winterbourne is not that sympathetic in the movie, I felt he was much more unsympathetic in the book.

He *was* more unsympathetic in the book. So was Giovanelli. I felt that Winterbourne was a man who's dying at the beginning of the story, and he lets himself die all the way, so that by the end there's no hope for him. It takes him a long time to die, and it only takes Daisy a reel. I found Winterbourne sad and pathetic. I couldn't hate him—although I tried to, because he stands for everything I loathe. He's a coward, he's a judge, he's mean-spirited.

Is it true that at one point you considered playing the Winterbourne role yourself?

Yes.

Why?

Because it's very difficult to find an actor in America who looks as though he has read a book. In the history of American movies there have been very few actors like that. Orson Welles had it, in a way Bogart had it, and Jimmy Stewart, when he was younger. Montgomery Clift had it—he would have been very good casting for the part of Winterbourne, except that he would have been a little bit *too* sensitive. But I can't think of a young actor in America today who gives you the feeling that he's read a book—whether he *has* or not.

Barry Brown *looks* as though he has—he looks intelligent. So do I, but I decided not to do the part and I'm glad I didn't.

The opening scene of the movie, with Randolph switching the shoes in the hotel corridor, is not in the book.

Well, Orson Welles once said to me, "If I were doing that picture, I'd begin with the little boy." And it stuck in my mind. So when I was discussing the script with Raphael, I quoted that line to him. He said, "Welles is a pretty good fellow to take a cue from, so why don't we do that?" And then we came up with the switching shoes business.

Except for Mrs. Walker, the boy is the character with whom you take the most liberties and improvise the most. He becomes more sinister and self-asserting than he is in the book.

Yes. I think one of the mistakes made with children in movies is that they're too sweet—something I tried to correct in *Paper Moon*. Children are not sweet—they're savages who are slowly being tamed to live in society. I think adorable children are either not real, or if they *are* real, you want to hit them.

I think in the book James starts Randolph off as a little bit more of a typical child—he's too sweet in the beginning of the story; then he changes, becomes nastier and funnier later. I think James never bothered to make him less sweet in the beginning, so we rewrote that and made him tougher.

I also liked the idea of there being this element of foreboding about Randolph, as if he somehow knows what's going to happen. Children do have, I think, a sixth sense, because they're closer to their feelings than adults. In a subtle way, I wanted Randolph to feel what was happening between Daisy and Winterbourne, which is why I added that abstracted little moment where he's up in the tree and goes "Bang" with the fake rifle after Winterbourne. Then, later, we see Randolph fooling around with a noose. Children are obsessed with death anyway—they're more ghoulish than grownups—and I think that fits in with the story. Of course, it all leads up to the final rejection of Winterbourne by Randolph, which was my idea of how to end the picture.

Yes, that's definitely different from the book, where you feel that Winterbourne is almost patronizing the child.

Yes, as he does everyone else in the story.

In the movie, the Miller family always talks very fast, almost comically so. Why did you do that?

Well, the story is full of these long, long speeches which were written by James as one huge paragraph. And it just seemed to me in reading them that that's the way they would sound: just rattling on quickly and talking about this and that. I also thought it would be funny if we meet Randolph and he talks fast, interrupts all the time, and then Daisy does it, and then the mother does it. So we finally realize where it all comes from—the mother. It's a rather amusing way of finding out that all these Millers just talk and interrupt, and they're all rude.

In the movie, our first introduction to Mrs. Costello, Winterbourne's aunt, is in a steambath.

That was Raphael's idea. I was nervous about it for a time, and the actress was very much against it. This was the first time that her character appeared, and Millie Natwick felt that there was no way that she could recover from the ridiculousness of that position —pouring tea in a bath. I felt that she had a point.

However, I finally decided it would be more effective if she *did* start out as a figure of fun, or at least a figure of more humor than she is in the original story, so that as the story got darker in Rome, there was a definite change. The only other way you could have shown her was in a hotel room in Vevey, and it would have been an awful lot like the scene in her room in Rome—closed, Victorian surroundings. I thought ultimately that when we see Mrs. Costello at the beginning, even *she* should be in a little more relaxed atmosphere than she is in Rome.

But when she says, "You've lived too long out of

the country. You'll be sure to make some great mistake"—which I think is a very important moment—I made sure that they were out of the bath. That's the main reason I had them get out at all.

A main difference between the movie and the book is that the movie is definitely more nostalgic. The idea of the lost moment is made much more explicit—for instance, in the Chillon scene, which you expanded and which ends with a very nostalgic shot of the castle receding through the carriage window.

Well, it was very important to me that Chillon be something that the audience remembers with some degree of pleasure. Did you like the man playing the harmonica in that scene? Some people think his music too mournful. I believe it has the advantage of making the sequence both present and past at the same time.

You see, there is this moment between Daisy and Winterbourne at Chillon, there's a possibility of something happening and it doesn't quite. Now, my feeling is that whenever there's a joyous time, there's also an inner knowledge that this time is going to end. The music gives you both things at once, because at the same time that everything they're doing is gay, the music is implying that this is going to be over. And when it's over, it will be in the past, something you remember with pleasure or regret.

The character of Mrs. Walker is somewhat changed from the book.

Yes, she's more sexual. In the story, she was the one character who seemed to me a bit ludicrous. I felt her motivation needed an edge to it because James doesn't explain why she is so upset by Daisy, except perhaps because of propriety, which I don't think is enough.

If I'd cast Mrs. Walker the way she was written, it would have been like that lady next door in Welles's

The Magnificent Ambersons, who tells Tim Holt,
"You'll be pleased to leave my house!" But Eileen
Brennan projects a quite sensual quality. And I
thought if she *played* the role very much the opposite,
it would be a wonderful contrast—this sort of sensu-
ality coming out underneath. Then we invented the
character of Charles, Winterbourne's friend, because I
thought it would be nice to show somebody whom
Mrs. Walker makes a pass at after she fails with Winterbourne.

*Throughout the Rome section, Daisy is associated with
mirrors.*

Well, you, being an old Douglas Sirk* fan, could probably tell me what that means more than I can. But one
of my reasons was that using mirrors would enable me
not to have to cut. It made things smoother because
I could show Winterbourne in closeup and also see
what he was looking at without having to cut to his
point of view.

But if you want to analyze it on a more dramatic
level, the mirrors tie in with the whole voyeuristic
aspect of Winterbourne: he'll look but he won't touch.
He'll examine with his eyes, but he won't make a move
to really grasp it, except perhaps obliquely. Even at
the Pincio, when he sees Daisy and Giovanelli behind
the parasol, you'll notice that the way he steps forward
is very much like a voyeur, he sort of tiptoes up, watching to see something, hoping that something terrible will
happen.

*There's a very mysterious moment in the Pincio scene,
when Winterbourne glimpses a lady in the background.
What was that?*

---

* Director of such films as *Tarnished Angels, Written on the
Wind, A Time to Love and A Time to Die,* and *Imitation of
Life.*

That was a remnant of something in Raphael's script that I thought worth keeping. She's an unattached woman, alone, obviously a whore or a loose woman. And she gives Winterbourne a look. He notices her—he's afraid to look at her, but he's interested, he's tempted. I thought it was necessary to show just a little bit of his sexuality and his hypocrisy—he's tempted by her just as he's tempted by Daisy in another way. It's just one of those small ambiguous moments of which the story is so full. And I also liked what happened in the Punch and Judy show during that scene.

Why did you put that in?

It was Raphael's idea, but if you've been at all to the Pincio in Rome, it's the thing you would naturally think of for atmosphere because there is a Punch and Judy show there, and it's probably been there for hundreds of years. The man we found who did it was remarkable and I just photographed his act and used the parts of it I thought most appropriate. What I particularly liked was the moment when Punch slays Death. I thought that was interesting, particularly in relation to how Daisy reacts to it: she just laughs, and they all laugh. It's wonderful, the idea of Punch slaying Death; it's a sort of comic contradiction of the ending.

There's also a parallel in the music when Winterbourne learns of Daisy's death—it brings back the atmosphere of the Pincio.

Yes, I used that same organ-grinder music—"La Donna e Mobile" from Verdi—three times in the picture. The first time is when we first see Rome outside of Mrs. Costello's window, and then at the Pincio, and then when he hears of her death. Each time it's a little louder, a little closer. The song actually, if you want to get into it, is from *Rigoletto,* and it's also used there two or three times. The last time, it's heard off-scene while this terrible, tragic scene happens on-stage.

The photographic style of Daisy Miller *is much more painterly than in any of your other films. Was there any particular painter you had in mind?*

My father, if anyone. He was very influenced by the French school, particularly the Impressionists, and yet he came from a Byzantine tradition, which means his colors were far more vivid and vibrant.

By the way, I think it's also very important to remember that this is the first movie I've made in which the time period of the story exists prior to the invention of movies.

No marquees in the background.

Definitely not. All my other movies were set in a time when movies were a part of what people did. I think movies have had a tremendous influence not only on me but on the characters in my movies, on life in general. But since *Daisy Miller* exists in a time when there were no movies, I thought it was especially important that this be the simplest movie in terms of the way it's shot. There's very little attempt to be in any way what is called "cinematic." I don't ever try to be, but in this one I tried to be even less.

How did you feel about the use of the Roman fever in the narrative? Did you ever feel uncomfortable with it? In the book it struck me as a little too deus ex machina.

Well, I thought it had to be very carefully set up; otherwise we would be in a lot of trouble. There was, in fact, a Roman fever, which was malaria—malaria is Italian and means literally "bad air," *mal aria.* At that time, it was something you caught if you went to the Colosseum or places like that, which in those days were near the swamps. But I still tried to prepare the audience for it as much as possible—for instance, when Daisy says, "I guess we'll stay all winter if we don't die of the fever!" Of course, James tries to prepare you for it too.

But was this the only thing that could happen when one went to Rome? It's like someone going to New York City and saying, "I guess I'll stay all winter if I don't get mugged and raped in Central Park," and then they get mugged and raped in Central Park. The End.

Well, I was aware that it might appear that way to a modern audience, but I liked it. It's not necessarily realistic—rather a symbol in James's mind for the stuffiness and the bad air of the Old World, which kills off the New World. On the other hand, there was an outbreak of cholera while we were in Rome and tourists stayed away in droves and it's all anyone talked about—and a bunch of people died from it. Now this is a hundred years later in the history of medicine, so perhaps we are underestimating the danger of the fever in its day.

Of course, James was very ambiguous about the Old World-New World business. Personally I'm not sure it's the Old World killing off the New, but it's a complicated point. I was going to say that America obviously has vulgarized a great part of the Old World. Whether or not that's something bad, we can't say yet. Certainly we've brought a vitality that was important—new air and vigor. I think for the first fifty years of this century, the American influence in Europe and the world has been positive. Whether or not it has been for the last twenty-five years, I don't know. But it is true that the New World brought a sense of vitality and life, which Daisy symbolizes. I think the picture as it's made is generally rather pro-American.

When Pete Hamill saw the film, he said it looked

to him as if Henry James had been rewritten by Mark Twain—it does have somewhat more of an energetic American quality than James's story. On the other hand, a French critic for *Elle* said that it was a completely European film—she couldn't imagine that an American had made it.

That's one of the things that confuse critics about me—they forget that I have a European heritage. Although my parents were living in America, I was brought up in a household that was completely European rather than American. In fact, I learned to speak Serbian before I spoke English. I think that's one of the big dualities in me. Although I embraced and continue to embrace America, very much like a first-generation American, I do have an artistic background which is totally European—my father being a Serbian painter, and my mother a Viennese.

Not just you—one of the curiosities of American film history is that it seems like half the directors have foreign backgrounds—Hitchcock, Lang, Lubitsch, Von Stroheim, Kazan, Chaplin, Borzage, and so on.

It's true, but then that's part of American history too. As Hitchcock once said to me, "America is full of foreigners." It's one of the reasons why American movies have always been the most universally appealing —because there's always been this mix. And it's what has kept them healthy, I think—until recently—perhaps we need some foreign blood.

Would you ever want to make a film about your background?

You mean like *The Quiet Man*—going back to the Old Sod. No, I haven't yet felt the urge. I don't know that I've come to terms with my own background. I just know that it must be what makes me feel out of step with so many other American filmmakers in my age category.

You've said that the final scene of the film presented the most problems.

Yes, it's the only thing that was changed four times in the cutting. The big problem is that the story is basically very subtle, very reserved, and yet we're stuck with an ending which I find terribly moving. To me, the powerful moment is when Randolph turns his back on Winterbourne—an idea I had long ago. I wanted the scene to be very smooth and quiet and simple—there's no cut up till then, when Randolph breaks it all. Because as far as Winterbourne is concerned, until that moment he can handle it all. He's upset by what Giovanelli tells him—"She did what she liked," and "She never would have married me." But it doesn't all come together until Randolph looks at him that way. I think it's the final moment of realization—something penetrates that thick skull.

The book ends with the implication that Winterbourne goes back to that woman in Geneva, but that's not really implied in the movie.

No, it isn't. I didn't see how to get that across in the movie. And I didn't really care about it that much. That's why the last shot leaves him where it does—in the graveyard. I think that's where he ends up, spiritually; it's all over.

It's a shot of paralysis, like the last shot of a Hitchcock film.

I suppose you're right—like the end of *Vertigo,* which I think is so intensely sad.

I find that some people react to this movie by not understanding Daisy almost as much as Winterbourne doesn't. I think that speaks well of the movie, actually, because it shows that Daisy's problem, and the problem of a girl like that, isn't confined to the nineteenth century. The movie could easily be a metaphor for a girl of today. In fact, if you care to look at it that way, it is. Women still don't have the freedom to be what that girl was. There's still a double standard in terms of how men deal with women and what they think about women—how easy it is for a man to put a woman down. Part of what I think is so reprehensible about Winterbourne is the fact that he thinks nothing of Daisy's so-called indiscretions when she's with *him*, it's only when she's with somebody else that he judges her as a loose woman.

Exactly. I don't know if that came out clearly enough in the movie, because in the book, when Winterbourne and Daisy go to Chillon, it's mentioned that people were looking at them. Then, when Daisy goes out on the Pincio to see Giovanelli, it's the same thing—everybody stares. And James writes that Winterbourne is "rather oddly rubbed the wrong way by this." What "oddly" refers to is: why should he be upset this time?

Yes. I didn't tell it that way. I decided not to tell it in terms of other people's reactions on the street. It seemed to me that Mrs. Walker was the one who was reacting badly, and if you generalized it, then it would become a social story, which I don't think is terribly interesting. If everybody is stopping to look at her, it becomes a story about how this just isn't done in this society. I don't think it's about society condemning her, it's about one or two people condemning her. I think that's always an easy way out, to say, "Well, society . . ." Society is made up of a bunch of people, and it's the one or two you know that screw you, not the whole world.

I also thought Winterbourne's hypocrisy is implicit in the way he behaves on the Pincio and before, when he asks her to go out on the lake with him in Switzerland. He's ready to take her out in the middle of the night, which is exactly what Giovanelli does at the Colosseum. I don't make too much of it, but I feel it's clear that Winterbourne is jealous as opposed to simply proper. Actually, James makes no mention of jealousy in the story.

A couple of friends of mine who have seen the film had, I thought, rather dense reactions. They said, "Well, gee, we didn't know until the last reel that she was really innocent." And I said, "But what does that matter?" I think it's a very important point to make that, as far as the director of the movie is concerned—I don't know about James—it's not important whether Daisy is, in fact, innocent. The fact that maybe she is, which is what Giovanelli tells Winterbourne, is an interesting point, but I don't think it matters. It's as though if she weren't innocent, then Winterbourne's reactions would be correct and justified.

It's like making a movie against capital punishment, and the man who's going to be executed is innocent. The point is not well made then because it becomes a story about a man who's unjustly murdered for something he didn't do. If you're going to make a plea against capital punishment, the man has to be guilty as hell. *That's* the point. So if you're making a movie about a girl who's a flirt—who, as Giovanelli says at the end, "did what she liked"—then it isn't a question of whether she is innocent or not. We're saying, "Why shouldn't she do what she likes?"

*   *   *

Martin Rubin received his B.A. in 1969 from Yale University, where he was chairman of the Yale Film Society. He collaborated with Eric Sherman on a collection of interviews entitled **The Director's Event** (Atheneum, 1970), and was managing editor and executive editor of the short-lived magazine **On Film.** He has contributed interviews and articles to the **Village Voice, Real Paper, Movie Magazine, New Journal, Film Comment,** and the anthology **Favorite Films.** Since 1972 he has been Film Program Director of the New York Cultural Center, and he was special assistant to the director of the San Francisco Film Festival in 1973.

DAISY MILLER

PREFACE

by Henry James[1]

IT WAS in Rome during the autumn of 1877; a friend
then living there but settled now in a South less
weighted with appeals and memories happened to mention—which she might perfectly not have done—some
simple and uninformed American lady of the previous
winter, whose young daughter, a child of nature and of
freedom, accompanying her from hotel to hotel, had
"picked up" by the wayside, with the best conscience
in the world, a good-looking Roman, of vague identity,
astonished at his luck, yet (so far as might be, by the
pair) all innocently, all serenely exhibited and introduced: this at least till the occurrence of some small
social check, some interrupting incident, of no great
gravity or dignity, and which I forget. I had never
heard, save on this showing, of the amiable but not
otherwise eminent ladies, who weren't in fact named,
I think, and whose case had merely served to point a
familiar moral; and it must have been just their want
of salience that left a margin for the small pencil-mark
inveterately signifying, in such connexions, "Dramatise,
dramatise!" The result of my recognising a few months
later the sense of my pencil-mark was the short chron-
icle of "Daisy Miller," which I indited in London the

[1] Written for the 1909 New York edition of his work.

following spring and then addressed, with no conditions attached, as I remember, to the editor of a magazine that had its seat of publication at Philadelphia and had lately appeared to appreciate my contributions. That gentleman[1] however (an historian of some repute) promptly returned me my missive, and with an absence of comment that struck me at the time as rather grim—as, given the circumstances, requiring indeed some explanation: till a friend to whom I appealed for light, giving him the thing to read, declared it could only have passed with the Philadelphian critic for "an outrage on American girlhood." This was verily a light, and of bewildering intensity; though I was presently to read into the matter a further helpful inference. To the fault of being outrageous this little composition added that of being essentially and pre-eminently a *nouvelle;* a signal example in fact of that type, foredoomed at the best, in more cases than not, to editorial disfavour. If accordingly I was afterwards to be cradled, almost blissfully, in the conception that "Daisy" at least, among my productions, might approach "success," such for example, on her eventual appearance, as the state of being promptly pirated in Boston—a sweet tribute I hadn't yet received and was never again to know—the irony of things yet claimed its rights, I couldn't but long continue to feel, in the circumstance that quite a special reprobation had waited on the first appearance in the world of the ultimately most prosperous child of my invention. So doubly discredited, at all events, this bantling met indulgence, with no great delay, in the eyes of my admirable friend the late Leslie Stephen and was published in two numbers of "The Cornhill Magazine" (1878).[2]

[1] It was John Foster Kirk, editor of *Lippincott's* from 1870 to 1886.

[2] Shortly after its appearance in this English magazine, pirated versions of the story sprang up in America in *Living Age* (Boston) and *Home Journal* (New York).

It qualified itself in that publication and afterwards as "a Study"; for reasons which I confess I fail to recapture unless they may have taken account simply of a certain flatness in my poor little heroine's literal denomination. Flatness indeed, one must have felt, was the very sum of her story; so that perhaps after all the attached epithet was meant but as a deprecation, addressed to the reader, of any great critical hope of stirring scenes. It provided for mere concentration, and on an object scant and superficially vulgar—from which, however, a sufficiently brooding tenderness might eventually extract a shy incongruous charm. I suppress at all events here the appended qualification—in view of the simple truth, which ought from the first to have been apparent to me, that my little exhibition is made to no degree whatever in critical but, quite inordinately and extravagantly, in poetical terms. It comes back to me that I was at a certain hour long afterwards to have reflected, in this connexion, on the characteristic free play of the whirligig of time. It was in Italy again—in Venice and in the prized society of an interesting friend, now dead, with whom I happened to wait, on the Grand Canal, at the animated water-steps of one of the hotels. The considerable little terrace there was so disposed as to make a salient stage for certain demonstrations on the part of two young girls, children *they*, if ever, of nature and of freedom, whose use of those resources, in the general public eye, and under our own as we sat in the gondola, drew from the lips of a second companion, sociably afloat with us, the remark that there before us, with no sign absent, were a couple of attesting Daisy Millers. Then it was that, in my charming hostess's prompt protest, the whirligig, as I have called it, at once betrayed itself. "How can you liken *those* creatures to a figure of which the only fault is touchingly to have transmuted so sorry a type and to have, by a poetic artifice, not only led our judgement of it astray, but made *any* judgement quite impossible?" With which this gentle lady and admirable critic turned on the author himself. "You *know* you quite falsified, by the turn you gave it, the thing you had begun with having in mind, the thing you had had, to satiety, the chance of 'observing': your pretty perversion of it, or your unprincipled mystification of our sense of it, does it really too much honour —in spite of which, none the less, as anything charming or touching always to that extent justifies itself, we after a fashion forgive and understand you. But why *waste* your romance? There are cases, too many, in which you've done it again; in which, provoked by a spirit of observation at first no doubt sufficiently sincere, and with the measured and felt truth fairly twitching your sleeve, you have yielded to your incurable prejudice in favour of grace—to whatever it is in you that makes so inordinately for form and prettiness and pathos; not to say sometimes for misplaced drolling. Is it that you've after all too much imagination? Those awful young women capering at the hotel-door, *they* are the real little Daisy Millers that were; whereas yours in the tale is such a one, more's the pity, as—for pitch of the ingenuous, for quality of the artless—couldn't possibly have been at all." My answer to all which bristled of course with more professions than I can or need report here; the chief of them inevitably to the effect that my supposedly typical little figure was of course pure poetry, and had never been anything else; since this is what helpful imagination, in however slight a dose, ever directly makes for. As for the original grossness of readers, I dare say I added, that was another matter—but one which at any rate had then quite ceased to signify.

Note: In writing the screenplay for **Daisy Miller,** both of Henry James's versions of the story—the 1878 original and the 1909 revision—were used. I found that whereas the descriptive sections were almost invariably better in the later draft, the dialogue was sometimes simpler and therefore more natural in the first. For this edition, therefore, though the main text follows the 1909 rewrite, we have footnoted those excerpts from the 1878 version that were valuable for the film or that might be of general interest in showing James's evolution as a stylist over a period of thirty years. My thanks to Mae Woods, who prepared this for publication, with the assistance of William Shepherd.

P.B.

DAISY MILLER[1]

I

AT THE LITTLE TOWN of Vevey, in Switzerland, there is a particularly comfortable hotel; there are indeed many hotels, since the entertainment of tourists is the business of the place, which, as many travellers will remember, is seated upon the edge of a remarkably blue lake—a lake that it behoves every tourist to visit. The shore of the lake presents an unbroken array of establishments of this order, of every category, from the "grand hotel" of the newest fashion, with a chalk-white front, a hundred balconies, and a dozen flags flying from its roof, to the small Swiss pension of an elder day, with its name inscribed in German-looking lettering upon a pink or yellow wall and an awkward summer-house in the angle of the garden. One of the hotels at Vevey, however, is famous, even classical, being distinguished from many of its upstart neighbours by an air both of luxury and of maturity. In this region, through the month of June, American travellers are extremely numerous; it may be said indeed that Vevey assumes

[1] Originally: *Daisy Miller: A Study.*

at that time some of the characteristics of an American watering-place. There are sights and sounds that evoke a vision, an echo, of Newport and Saratoga. There is a flitting hither and thither of "stylish" young girls, a rustling of muslin flounces, a rattle of dance-music in the morning hours, a sound of high-pitched voices at all times. You receive an impression of these things at the excellent inn of the "Trois Couronnes," and are transported in fancy to the Ocean House or to Congress Hall. But at the "Trois Couronnes," it must be added, there are other features much at variance with these suggestions: neat German waiters who look like secretaries of legation; Russian princesses sitting in the garden; little Polish boys walking about, held by the hand, with their governors; a view of the snowy crest of the Dent du Midi and the picturesque towers of the Castle of Chillon.

I hardly know whether it was the analogies or the differences that were uppermost in the mind of a young American, who, two or three years ago, sat in the garden of the "Trois Couronnes," looking about him rather idly at some of the graceful objects I have mentioned. It was a beautiful summer morning, and in whatever fashion the young American looked at things they must have seemed to him charming. He had come from Geneva the day before, by the little steamer, to see his aunt, who was staying at the hotel—Geneva having been for a long time his place of residence. But his aunt had a headache—his aunt had almost always a headache—and she was now shut up in her room smelling camphor, so that he was at liberty to wander about. He was some seven-and-twenty years of age; when his friends spoke of him they usually said that he was at Geneva "studying." When his enemies spoke of him they said—but after all he had no enemies: he was extremely amiable and generally liked. What I should say is simply that when certain persons spoke of him they conveyed that the reason of his spending so much time at Geneva was that he was extremely devoted to a lady who lived there—a foreign lady, a person older than himself. Very few Americans —truly I think none—had ever seen this lady, about whom there were some singular stories. But Winterbourne had an old attachment for the little capital of Calvinism; he had been put to school there as a boy and had afterwards even gone, on trial—trial of the grey old "Academy" on the steep and stony hillside —to college there; circumstances which had led to his forming a great many youthful friendships. Many of these he had kept, and they were a source of great satisfaction to him.

After knocking at his aunt's door and learning that she was indisposed he had taken a walk about the town and then he had come in to his breakfast. He had now finished that repast, but was enjoying a small cup of coffee which had been served him on a little table in the garden by one of the waiters who looked like *attachés*. At last he finished his coffee and lit a cigarette. Presently a small boy came walking along the path—an urchin of nine or ten. The child, who was diminutive for his years, had an aged expression of countenance, a pale complexion and sharp little features. He was dressed in knickerbockers and had red stockings that displayed his poor little spindle-shanks; he also wore a brilliant red cravat. He carried in his hand a long alpenstock, the sharp point of which he thrust into everything he approached—the flower-beds, the garden-benches, the trains of the ladies' dresses. In front of Winterbourne he paused, looking at him with a pair of bright and penetrating little eyes.

"Will you give me a lump of sugar?" he asked in a small sharp hard voice—a voice immature and yet somehow not young.

Winterbourne glanced at the light table near him, on which his coffee-service rested, and saw that several morsels of sugar remained. "Yes, you may take one," he answered; "but I don't think too much sugar good for little boys."

This little boy stepped forward and carefully selected three of the coveted fragments, two of which he buried in the pocket of his knickerbockers, depositing the other as promptly in another place. He poked his alpenstock, lance-fashion, into Winterbourne's bench and tried to crack the lump of sugar with his teeth.

"Oh blazes; it's har-r-d!" he exclaimed, divesting vowel and consonants, pertinently enough, of any taint of softness.

Winterbourne had immediately gathered that he might have the honour of claiming him as a country-man. "Take care you don't hurt your teeth," he said paternally.

"I haven't got any teeth to hurt. They've all come out. I've only got seven teeth. Mother counted them last night, and one came out right afterwards. She said she'd slap me if any more came out. I can't help it. It's this old Europe. It's the climate that makes them come out. In America they didn't come out. It's these hotels."

Winterbourne was much amused. "If you eat three lumps of sugar your mother will certainly slap you," he ventured.

"She's got to give me some candy then," rejoined his young interlocutor. "I can't get any candy here— any American candy. American candy's the best candy."

"And are American little boys the best little boys?" Winterbourne asked.

"I don't know. *I'm* an American boy," said the child.

"I see you're one of the best!" the young man laughed.

"Are you an American man?" pursued this vivacious infant. And then on his friend's affirmative reply, "American men are the best," he declared with as-surance.

His companion thanked him for the compliment, and the child, who had now got astride of his alpenstock, stood looking about him while he attacked another lump of sugar. Winterbourne wondered if he himself had been like this in his infancy, for he had been brought to Europe at about the same age.

"Here comes my sister!" cried his young compatriot. "She's an American girl, you bet!"

Winterbourne looked along the path and saw a beautiful young lady advancing. "American girls are the best girls," he thereupon cheerfully remarked to his visitor.

"My sister ain't the best!" the child promptly returned. "She's always blowing at me."

"I imagine that's your fault, not hers," said Winterbourne. The young lady meanwhile had drawn near. She was dressed in white muslin, with a hundred frills and flounces and knots of pale-coloured ribbon. Bareheaded, she balanced in her hand a large parasol with a deep border of embroidery; and she was strikingly, admirably pretty. "How pretty they are!" thought our friend, who straightened himself in his seat as if he were ready to rise.

The young lady paused in front of his bench, near the parapet of the garden, which overlooked the lake. The small boy had now converted his alpenstock into a vaulting-pole, by the aid of which he was springing about in the gravel and kicking it up not a little. "Why, Randolph," she freely began, "what *are* you doing?"

"I'm going up the Alps!" cried Randolph. "This is the way!" And he gave another extravagant jump, scattering the pebbles about Winterbourne's ears.

"That's the way they come down," said Winterbourne.

"He's an American man!" proclaimed Randolph in his harsh little voice.

The young lady gave no heed to this circumstance, but looked straight at her brother. "Well, I guess you'd better be quiet," she simply observed.

It seemed to Winterbourne that he had been in a manner presented. He got up and stepped slowly toward the charming creature, throwing away his cig-

arette. "This little boy and I have made acquaintance,"
he said with great civility. In Geneva, as he had been
perfectly aware, a young man wasn't at liberty to speak
to a young unmarried lady save under certain rarely-
occurring conditions; but here at Vevey what conditions could be better than these?—a pretty American
girl coming to stand in front of you in a garden with
all the confidence in life. This pretty American girl,
whatever that might prove, on hearing Winterbourne's
observation simply glanced at him; she then turned her
head and looked over the parapet, at the lake and the
opposite mountains. He wondered whether he had
gone too far, but decided that he must gallantly advance
rather than retreat. While he was thinking of something else to say the young lady turned again to the
little boy, whom she addressed quite as if they were
alone together. "I should like to know where you got
that pole."

"I bought it!" Randolph shouted.

"You don't mean to say you're going to take it to
Italy!"

"Yes, I'm going to take it t' Italy!" the child rang
out.

She glanced over the front of her dress and
smoothed out a knot or two of ribbon. Then she gave
her sweet eyes to the prospect again. "Well, I guess
you'd better leave it somewhere," she dropped after a
moment.

"Are you going to Italy?" Winterbourne now decided
very respectfully to enquire.

She glanced at him with lovely remoteness. "Yes,
sir," she then replied. And she said nothing more.

["And are you—a—thinking of the Simplon?" he
pursued with a slight drop of assurance.][2]

"I don't know," she said. "I suppose it's some mountain. Randolph, what mountain are we thinking of?"

---

[2] "Are you—a—going over the Simplon?" Winterbourne pursued, a little embarrassed.

"Thinking of?"—the boy stared.

"Why going right over."

"Going to where?" he demanded.

"Why right down to Italy"—Winterbourne felt vague emulations.

"I don't know," said Randolph. "I don't want to go t' Italy. I want to go to America."

"Oh Italy's a beautiful place!" the young man laughed.

"Can you get candy there?" [Randolph asked of all the echoes.][3]

"I hope not," said his sister. "I guess you've had enough candy, and mother thinks so too."

"I haven't had any for ever so long—for a hundred weeks!" cried the boy, still jumping about.

The young lady inspected her flounces and smoothed her ribbons again; and Winterbourne presently risked an observation on the beauty of the view. He was ceasing to be [in doubt,][4] for he had begun to perceive that she was really not in the least embarrassed. She might be cold, she might be austere, she might even be prim; for that was apparently—he had already so generalised—what the most "distant" American girls did: they came and planted themselves straight in front of you to show how rigidly unapproachable they were. There hadn't been the slightest flush in her fresh fairness however; so that she was clearly neither offended nor fluttered. Only she was composed—he had seen that before too—of charming little parts that didn't match and that made no *ensemble;* and if she looked another way when he spoke to her, and seemed not particularly to hear him, this was simply her habit, her manner, the result of her having no idea whatever of "form" (with such a tell-tale appendage as Randolph where in the world would she have got it?) in any such connexion. As he talked a little more and pointed out

[3] Randolph loudly inquired.
[4] embarrassed

some of the objects of interest in the view, with which
she appeared wholly unacquainted, she gradually, none
the less, gave him more of the benefit of her attention;
and then he saw that [act unqualified by the faintest
shadow of reserve. It wasn't however what would have
been called a "bold" front that she presented, for her
expression was as decently limpid as the very cleanest
water.]⁵ Her eyes were the very prettiest conceivable,
and indeed Winterbourne hadn't for a long time seen
anything prettier than his fair countrywoman's various
features—her complexion, her nose, her ears, her teeth.
[He took a great interest generally in that range of
effects and was addicted to noting and, as it were, re-
cording them;]⁶ so that in regard to this young lady's
face he made several observations. It wasn't at all insip-
id, yet at the same time wasn't pointedly—what point,
on earth, could she ever make?—expressive; and though
it offered such a collection of small finenesses and neat-
nesses he mentally accused it—very forgivingly—of a
want of finish. [He thought nothing more likely than
that its wearer would have had her own experience of
the action of her charms, as she would certainly have
acquired a resulting confidence;]⁷ but even should she
depend on this for her main amusement her bright
sweet superficial little visage gave out neither mockery
nor irony. Before long it became clear that, however
these things might be, she was much disposed to conversation. She remarked to Winterbourne that they were
going to Rome for the winter—she and her mother and
Randolph. She asked him if he was a "real American";
she wouldn't have taken him for one; he seemed more
like a German—[this flower was gathered as from a large

⁵ this glance was perfectly direct and unshrinking. It was
not, however, what would have been called an immodest glance,
for the young girl's eyes were singularly honest and fresh.
⁶ He had a great relish for feminine beauty; he was addicted
to observing and analyzing it;
⁷ He thought it very possible that Master Randolph's sister
was a coquette; he was sure she had a spirit of her own;

field of comparison]⁸—especially when he spoke. Winterbourne, laughing, answered that he had met Germans who spoke like Americans, but not, so far as he remembered, any American with the resemblance she noted. Then he asked her if she mightn't be more at ease should she occupy the bench he had just quitted. She answered that she liked hanging round, but she none the less resignedly, after a little, dropped to the bench. She told him she was from New York State—"if you know where that is"; but our friend really quickened this current by catching hold of her small slippery brother and making him stand a few minutes by his side.

"Tell me your honest name, my boy." So he artfully proceeded.

In response to which the child was indeed unvarnished truth. "Randolph C. Miller. And I'll tell you hers." With which he levelled his alpenstock at his sister.

"You had better wait till you're asked!" said this young lady quite at her leisure.

"I should like very much to know *your* name," Winterbourne made free to reply.

"Her name's Daisy Miller!" cried the urchin. "But that ain't her real name; that ain't her name on her cards."

"It's a pity you haven't got one of my cards!" Miss Miller quite as naturally remarked.

"Her real name's Annie P. Miller," the boy went on.

It seemed, all amazingly, to do her good. "Ask him *his* now"—and she indicated their friend.

But to this point Randolph seemed perfectly indifferent; he continued to supply information with regard to his own family. "My father's name is Ezra B. Miller. My father ain't in Europe—he's in a better place than Europe." Winterbourne for a moment supposed this the manner in which the child had been taught to intimate

---

⁸ this was said after a little hesitation

that Mr. Miller had been removed to the sphere of celestial rewards. But Randolph immediately added: "My father's in Schenectady. He's got a big business. My father's rich, you bet."

"Well!" ejaculated Miss Miller, lowering her parasol and looking at the embroidered border. Winterbourne presently released the child, who departed, dragging his alpenstock along the path. "He don't like Europe," said the girl as with an artless instinct for historic truth. "He wants to go back."

"To Schenectady, you mean?"

"Yes, he wants to go right home. He hasn't got any boys here. There's one boy here, but he always goes round with a teacher. They won't let him play."

"And your brother hasn't any teacher?" Winterbourne enquired.

It tapped, at a touch, the spring of confidence. "Mother thought of getting him one—to travel round with us. There was a lady told her of a very good teacher; an American lady—perhaps you know her— Mrs. Sanders. I think she came from Boston. She told her of this teacher, and we thought of getting him to travel round with us. But Randolph said he didn't want a teacher travelling round with us. He said he wouldn't have lessons when he was in the cars. And we *are* in the cars about half the time. There was an English lady we met in the cars—I think her name was Miss Featherstone; perhaps you know her. She wanted to know why I didn't give Randolph lessons—give him 'instruction,' she called it. I guess he could give me more instruction than I could give him. He's very smart."

"Yes," said Winterbourne; "he seems very smart."

"Mother's going to get a teacher for him as soon as we get t' Italy. Can you get good teachers in Italy?"

"Very good, I should think," Winterbourne hastened to reply.

"Or else she's going to find some school. He ought to learn some more. He's only nine. He's going to college." And in this way Miss Miller continued to converse upon the affairs of her family and upon other topics. She sat there with her extremely pretty hands, ornamented with very brilliant rings, folded in her lap, and with her pretty eyes now resting upon those of Winterbourne, now wandering over the garden, the people who passed before her and the beautiful view. She addressed her new acquaintance as if she had known him a long time. He found it very pleasant. It was many years since he had heard a young girl talk so much. It might have been said of this wandering maiden who had come and sat down beside him upon a bench that she chattered. She was very quiet, she sat in a charming tranquil attitude; but her lips and her eyes were constantly moving. She had a soft slender agreeable voice, and her tone was distinctly sociable. She gave Winterbourne a report of her movements and intentions, and those of her mother and brother, in Europe, and enumerated in particular the various hotels at which they had stopped. "That English lady in the cars," she said —"Miss Featherstone—asked me if we didn't all live in hotels in America. I told her I had never been in so many hotels in my life as since I came to Europe. I've never seen so many—it's nothing but hotels." But Miss Miller made this remark with no querulous accent; she appeared to be in the best humour with everything. She declared that the hotels were very good when once you got used to their ways and that Europe was perfectly [entrancing.]⁹ She wasn't disappointed—not a bit. Perhaps it was because she had heard so much about it before. She had ever so many intimate friends who had been there ever so many times, and that way she had got thoroughly posted. And then she had had ever so many dresses and things from Paris. Whenever she put on a Paris dress she felt as if she were in Europe.

"It was a kind of a wishing-cap," Winterbourne smiled.

"Yes," said Miss Miller at once and without examin-

⁹ sweet.

ing this analogy; "it always made me wish I was here. But I needn't have done that for dresses. I'm sure they send all the pretty ones to America; you see the most frightful things here. The only thing I don't like," she proceeded, "is the society. There ain't any society—or if there is I don't know where it keeps itself. Do you? I suppose there's some society somewhere, but I haven't seen anything of it. I'm very fond of society and I've always had plenty of it. I don't mean only in Schenectady, but in New York. I used to go to New York every winter. In New York I had lots of society. Last winter I had seventeen dinners given me, and three of them were by gentlemen," added Daisy Miller. "I've more friends in New York than in Schenectady—more gentlemen friends; and more young lady friends too," she resumed in a moment. She paused again for an instant; she was looking at Winterbourne with all her prettiness in her frank gay eyes and in her clear rather uniform smile. "I've always had," she said, "a great deal of gentlemen's society."

Poor Winterbourne was amused and perplexed—above all he was charmed. He had never yet heard a young girl express herself in just this fashion; never at least save in cases where to say such things [was to have at the same time some rather complicated consciousness about them.][10] And yet was he to accuse Miss Daisy Miller of an actual or a potential *arrière-pensée,* as they said at Geneva? He felt he had lived at Geneva so long as to have got morally muddled; he had lost the right sense for the young American tone. Never indeed since he had grown old enough to appreciate things had he encountered a young compatriot of so "strong" a type as this. Certainly she was very charming, but how [extraordinarily communicative and how tremendously easy!][11] Was she simply a pretty girl from New York

[10] seemed a kind of demonstrative evidence of a certain laxity of deportment.
[11] deucedly sociable!

State—were they all like that, the pretty girls who had had a good deal of gentlemen's society? Or was she also a designing, an audacious, [in short an expert young person? Yes, his instinct for such a question had ceased to serve him, and his reason could but mislead.][12] Miss Daisy Miller looked extremely innocent. Some people had told him that after all American girls *were* exceedingly innocent, and others had told him that after all they weren't. He must on the whole take Miss Daisy Miller for a flirt—a pretty American flirt. He had never as yet had relations with representatives of that class. He had known here in Europe two or three women—persons older than Miss Daisy Miller and provided, for respectability's sake, with husbands—who were great coquettes; dangerous terrible women with whom one's light commerce might indeed take a serious turn. But this charming apparition wasn't a coquette in that sense; she was very unsophisticated; she was only a pretty American flirt. Winterbourne was almost grateful for having found the formula that applied to Miss Daisy Miller. He leaned back in his seat; he remarked to himself that she had the finest little nose he had ever seen; he wondered what were the regular conditions and limitations of one's intercourse with a pretty American flirt. It presently became apparent that he was on the way to learn.

"Have you been to that old castle?" the girl soon asked, pointing with her parasol to the far-shining walls of the Château de Chillon.

"Yes, formerly, more than once," said Winterbourne. "You too, I suppose, have seen it?"

"No, we haven't been there. I want to go there dreadfully. Of course I mean to go there. I wouldn't go away from here without having seen that old castle."

"It's a very pretty excursion," the young man re-

[12] an unscrupulous young person? Winterbourne had lost his instinct in this matter, and his reason could not help him.

turned, "and very easy to make. You can drive, you know, or you can go by the little steamer."

"You can go in the cars," said Miss Miller.

"Yes, you can go in the cars," Winterbourne assented.

"Our courier says they take you right up to the castle," she continued. "We were going last week, but mother gave out. She suffers dreadfully from dyspepsia. She said she couldn't any more go—!" But this sketch of Mrs. Miller's plea remained unfinished. "Randolph wouldn't go either; he says he don't think much of old castles. But I guess we'll go this week if we can get Randolph."

"Your brother isn't interested in ancient monuments?" [Winterbourne indulgently asked.][13]

He now drew her, as he guessed she would herself have said, every time. "Why no, he says he don't care much about old castles. He's only nine. He wants to stay at the hotel. Mother's afraid to leave him alone, and the courier won't stay with him; so we haven't been to many places. But it will be too bad if we don't go up there." And Miss Miller pointed again at the Château de Chillon.

"I should think it might be arranged," Winterbourne was thus emboldened to reply. "Couldn't you get some one to stay—for the afternoon—with Randolph?"

Miss Miller looked at him a moment, and then with all serenity, "I wish *you'd* stay with him!" she said.

[He pretended to consider it.][14] "I'd much rather go to Chillon with you."

"With me?" she asked without a shadow of emotion.

She didn't rise blushing, as a young person at Geneva would have done; and yet, [conscious that he had gone very far, he thought it possible she had drawn back.][15] "And with your mother," he answered very respectfully.

[13] Winterbourne inquired, smiling.

[14] Winterbourne hesitated a moment.

[15] conscious that he had been very bold, thought it possible she was offended.

But it seemed that both his audacity and his respect were lost on Miss Daisy Miller. "I guess mother wouldn't go—for *you*," she smiled. "And she ain't much *bent* on going, anyway. She don't like to ride round in the afternoon." After which she familiarly proceeded: "But did you really mean what you said just now—that you'd like to go up there?"

"Most earnestly I meant it," Winterbourne declared.

"Then we may arrange it. If mother will stay with Randolph I guess Eugenio will."

"Eugenio?" the young man echoed.

"Eugenio's our courier. He doesn't like to stay with Randolph—he's the most fastidious man I ever saw. But he's a splendid courier. I guess he'll stay at home with Randolph if mother does, and then we can go to the castle."

Winterbourne reflected for an instant as lucidly as possible: "we" could only mean Miss Miller and himself. This prospect seemed almost too good to believe; he felt as if he ought to kiss the young lady's hand. Possibly he would have done so,—and quite spoiled his chance; but at this moment another person—presumably Eugenio—appeared. A tall handsome man, with superb whiskers and wearing a velvet morning-coat and a [voluminous watch-guard,][16] approached the young lady, looking sharply at her companion. "Oh Eugenio!" she said with the friendliest accent.

Eugenio had eyed Winterbourne from head to foot; he now bowed gravely to Miss Miller. "I have the honour to inform Mademoiselle that luncheon's on table."

Mademoiselle slowly rose. "See here, Eugenio, I'm going to that old castle anyway."

"To the Château de Chillon, Mademoiselle?" the courier enquired. "Mademoiselle has made arrangements?" he added in a tone that struck Winterbourne as impertinent.

Eugenio's tone apparently threw, even to Miss Mil-

16 brilliant watch-chain

ler's own apprehension, a slightly ironical light on her position. She turned to Winterbourne with the slightest blush. "You won't back out?"

"I shall not be happy till we go!" he protested.

"And you're staying in this hotel?" she went on. "And you're really American?"

The courier still stood there with an effect of offense for the young man so far as the latter saw in it a tacit reflexion on Miss Miller's behaviour and an insinuation that she "picked up" acquaintances. "I shall have the honour of presenting to you a person who'll tell you all about me," he said, smiling, and referring to his aunt.

"Oh well, we'll go some day," she beautifully answered; with which she gave him a smile and turned away. She put up her parasol and walked back to the inn beside Eugenio. Winterbourne stood watching her, and as she moved away, drawing her muslin furbelows over the [walk,][17] he spoke to himself of her natural elegance.

II

HE HAD, however, engaged to do more than proved feasible in promising to present his aunt, Mrs. Costello, to Miss Daisy Miller. As soon as that lady had got better of her headache he waited on her in her apartment and, after a show of the proper solicitude about her health, asked if she had noticed in the hotel an American family—a mamma, a daughter and an obstreperous little boy.

"An obstreperous little boy and a preposterous big courier?" said Mrs. Costello. "Oh yes, I've noticed them. Seen them, heard them and kept out of their way." Mrs. Costello was a widow of fortune, a person of much distinction and who frequently intimated that

[17] gravel

if she hadn't been so dreadfully liable to sick-headaches she would probably have left a deeper impress on her time. She had a long pale face, a high nose and a great deal of very striking white hair, which she wore in large puffs [and]18 over the top of her head. She had two sons married in New York and another who was now in Europe. This young man was amusing himself at Homburg and, though guided by his taste, was rarely observed to visit any particular city at the moment selected by his mother for her appearance there. Her nephew, who had come to Vevey expressly to see her, was therefore more attentive than, as she said, her very own. He had imbibed at Geneva the idea that one must be irreproachable in all such forms. Mrs. Costello hadn't seen him for many years and was now greatly pleased with him, manifesting her approbation by initiating him into many of the secrets of that social sway which, as he could see she would like him to think, she exerted from her stronghold in Forty-Second Street. She admitted that she was very exclusive, but if he had been better acquainted with New York he would see that one had to be. And her picture of the minutely hierarchical constitution of the society of that city, which she presented to him in many different lights, was, to Winterbourne's imagination, almost oppressively striking.

He at once recognised from her tone that Miss Daisy Miller's place in the social scale was low. "I'm afraid you don't approve of them," he pursued in reference to his new friends.

"They're horribly common"—it was perfectly simple. "They're the sort of Americans that one does one's duty by just ignoring."

"Ah you just ignore them?"—the young man took it in.

"I can't *not,* my dear Frederick. I wouldn't if I hadn't to, but I have to."

18 and *rouleaux*

"The little girl's very pretty," he went on in a moment.

"Of course she's very pretty. But she's of the last crudity."

"I see what you mean of course," he allowed after another pause.

"She has that charming look they all have," his aunt resumed. "I can't think where they pick it up; and she dresses in perfection—no, you don't know how well she dresses. I can't think where they get their taste."

"But, my dear aunt, she's not, after all, a Comanche savage."

"She is a young lady," said Mrs. Costello, "who has an intimacy with her mamma's courier!"

["An 'intimacy' with him?" Ah there it was!][19]

"There's no other name for such a relation. But the skinny little mother's just as bad! They treat the courier as a familiar friend—as a gentleman and a scholar. I shouldn't wonder if he dines with them. Very likely they've never seen a man with such good manners, such fine clothes, so *like* a gentleman—or a scholar. He probably corresponds to the young lady's idea of a count. He sits with them in the garden of an evening. I think he smokes in their faces."

Winterbourne listened with interest to these disclosures; they helped him to make up his mind about Miss Daisy. Evidently she was rather wild. "Well," he said, "I'm not a courier and I didn't smoke in her face, and yet she was very charming to me."

"You had better have mentioned at first," Mrs. Costello returned with dignity, "that you had made her valuable acquaintance."

"We simply met in the garden and talked a bit."

"By appointment—no? Ah that's still to come! Pray what did you say?"

"I said I should take the liberty of introducing her to my admirable aunt."

[19] "An intimacy with the courier?" the young man demanded.

"Your admirable aunt's a thousand times obliged to you."

"It was to guarantee my respectability."

"And pray who's to guarantee hers?"

"Ah you're cruel!" said the young man. "She's a very innocent girl."

"You don't say that as if you believed it," Mrs. Costello returned.

"She's completely uneducated," Winterbourne acknowledged, "but she's wonderfully pretty, and in short she's very nice. To prove I believe it I'm going to take her to the Château de Chillon."

Mrs. Costello made a wondrous face. "You two are going off there together? I should say it proved just the contrary. How long had you known her, may I ask, when this interesting project was formed? You haven't been twenty-four hours in the house."

"I had known her half an hour!" Winterbourne smiled.

["Then she's just what I supposed."

"And what do you suppose?"

"Why that she's a horror."][20]

Our youth was silent for some moments. "You really think then," [he presently began,][21] and with a desire for trustworthy information, "you really think that—" But he paused again while his aunt waited.

"Think what, sir?"

"That she's the sort of young lady who expects a man sooner or later to—well, we'll call it carry her off?"

"I haven't the least idea what such young ladies expect a man to do. But I really consider you had better not meddle with little American girls who are uneducated, as you mildly put it. You've lived too long out of the country. You'll be sure to make some great mistake. You're too innocent."

20 "Dear me!" cried Mrs. Costello. "What a dreadful girl!"
21 he began, earnestly,

["My dear aunt, not so much as that comes to!" he protested with a laugh and a curl of his moustache.][22]

"You're too guilty then!"

He continued all thoughtfully to finger the ornament in question. "You won't let the poor girl know you then?" he asked at last.

"Is it literally true that she's going to the Château de Chillon with you?"

"I've no doubt she fully intends it."

"Then, my dear Frederick," said Mrs. Costello, "I must decline the honour of her acquaintance. I'm an old woman, but I'm not too old—thank heaven—to be honestly shocked!"

"But don't they all do these things—the little American girls at home?" Winterbourne enquired.

Mrs. Costello stared a moment. "I should like to see my granddaughters do them!" she then grimly returned.

This seemed to throw some light on the matter, for Winterbourne remembered to have heard his pretty cousins in New York, the daughters of this lady's two daughters, called "tremendous flirts." If therefore Miss Daisy Miller exceeded the liberal licence allowed to these young women [it was probable she did go even by the American allowance rather far.][23] Winterbourne was impatient to see her again, and it vexed, it even a little humiliated him, that he shouldn't by instinct appreciate her justly.

Though so impatient to see her again he hardly knew what ground he should give for his aunt's refusal to become acquainted with her; but he discovered promptly enough that with Miss Daisy Miller there was no great need of walking on tiptoe. He found her that evening in the garden, wandering about in the warm starlight after the manner of an indolent sylph and swinging to and fro the largest fan he had ever beheld. It was ten

[22] "My dear aunt, I am not so innocent," said Winterbourne, smiling and curling his moustache.

[23] it was probable that anything might be expected of her.

o'clock. He had dined with his aunt, had been sitting with her since dinner, and had just taken leave of her till the morrow. His young friend frankly rejoiced to renew their intercourse; she pronounced it the stupidest evening she had ever passed.

"Have you been all alone?" he asked with no intention of an epigram and no effect of her perceiving one.

"I've been walking round with mother. But mother gets tired walking round," Miss Miller explained.

"Has she gone to bed?"

"No, she doesn't like to go to bed. She doesn't sleep scarcely any—not three hours. She says she doesn't know how she lives. She's dreadfully nervous. I guess she sleeps more than she thinks. She's gone somewhere after Randolph; she wants to try to get him to go to bed. He doesn't like to go to bed."

The soft impartiality of her *constatations*, as Winterbourne would have termed them, was a thing by itself —exquisite little fatalist as they seemed to make her. "Let us hope she'll persuade him," he encouragingly said.

"Well, she'll talk to him all she can—but he doesn't like her to talk to him": with which Miss Daisy opened and closed her fan. "She's going to try to get Eugenio to talk to him. But Randolph ain't afraid of Eugenio. Eugenio's a splendid courier, but he can't make much impression on Randolph! I don't believe he'll go to bed before eleven." Her detachment from any invidious judgement of this was, to her companion's sense, inimitable; and it appeared that Randolph's vigil was in fact triumphantly prolonged, for Winterbourne attended her in her stroll for some time without meeting her mother. "I've been looking round for that lady you want to introduce me to," she resumed—"I guess she's your aunt." Then on his admitting the fact and expressing some curiosity as to how she had learned it, she said she had heard all about Mrs. Costello from the chambermaid. She was very quiet and very *comme il faut;* she wore white puffs; she spoke to no one and she

never dined at the common table. Every two days she
had a headache. "I think that's a lovely description,
headache and all!" said Miss Daisy, chattering along in
her thin gay voice. "I want to know her ever so much.
I know just what *your* aunt would be; I know I'd like
her. She'd be very exclusive. I like a lady to be exclusive; I'm dying to be exclusive myself. Well, I guess
we *are* exclusive, mother and I. We don't speak to any
one—or they don't speak to us. I suppose it's about the
same thing. Anyway, I shall be ever so glad to meet
your aunt."

Winterbourne was embarrassed—he could but trump
up some evasion. "She'd be most happy, but I'm afraid
those tiresome headaches are always to be reckoned
with."

The girl looked at him through the fine dusk.

"Well, I suppose she doesn't have a headache every
day."[24]

[He had to make the best of it. "She tells me she
wonderfully does." He didn't know what else to say.][25]

Miss Miller stopped and stood looking at him. Her
prettiness was still visible in the darkness; she kept
[flapping to and fro][26] her enormous fan. "She doesn't
want to know me!" she then lightly broke out. "Why
don't you say so? You needn't be afraid. *I'm* not
afraid!" And she quite crowed for the fun of it.

[Winterbourne distinguished, however, a wee false
note in this:][27] he was touched, shocked, mortified by
it. "My dear young lady, she knows no one. She goes
through life immured. It's her wretched health."

The young girl walked on a few steps in the glee of
the thing. "You needn't be afraid," she repeated. "Why
should she want to know me?" Then she paused again;
she was close to the parapet of the garden, and in front

[24] she said, sympathetically.
[25] Winterbourne was silent a moment. "She tells me she
does," he answered at last—not knowing what to say.
[26] opening and closing
[27] Winterbourne fancied there was a tremor in her voice;

Miss Annie P. "Daisy" Miller

RANDOLPH MILLER AND FREDERICK WINTERBOURNE

HOTEL TROIS COURONNES, VEVEY, SWITZERLAND

WINTERBOURNE MAKES THE ACQUAINTANCE OF

RANDOLPH AND HIS SISTER, DAISY MILLER

WINTERBOURNE AND HIS AUNT, MRS. COSTELLO

TAKING THE BATHS NEAR VEVEY

WINTERBOURNE MAKES THE ACQUAINTANCE

of Mrs. Ezra B. Miller, Daisy's mother

DAISY AND WINTERBOURNE TAKE A STEAMER

TO THE CHATEAU DE CHILLON

Daisy and Winterbourne

INSIDE THE CHATEAU

WINTERBOURNE IN ROME, AT MRS. COSTELLO'S APARTMENT

AND AT MRS. WALKER'S AFTERNOON TEA

At Mrs. Walker's tea, Winterbourne, Randolph,

DAISY, MRS. WALKER, AND MRS. MILLER

THE PUNCH AND JUDY SHOW AT

THE PINCIO PROMENADE, ROME

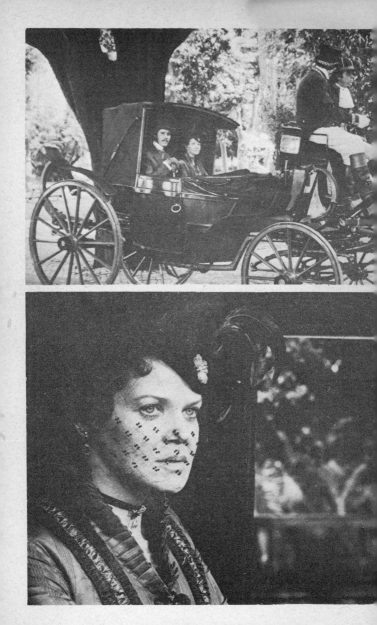

THE BORGHESE GARDENS, MRS. WALKER AND WINTERBOURNE

DAISY, WINTERBOURNE AND MR. GIOVANELLI

at Mrs. Walker's Party, Charles,

WINTERBOURNE, DAISY, GIOVANELLI, MRS. WALKER

DAISY AND GIOVANELLI

AT THE CHURCH

DAISY AND GIOVANELLI ARE SEEN ON THE CHURCH PIAZZA

THE MUSIC LESSON

THE COLOSSEUM, ROME

DAISY, WINTERBOURNE, GIOVANELLI

WINTERBOURNE LEARNS THAT DAISY IS GRAVELY ILL

DAISY'S FUNERAL, ROME

Frederick Forsyth Winterbourne

of her was the starlit lake. There was a vague sheen on
its surface, and in the distance were dimly-seen mountain forms. Daisy Miller looked out at these great lights
and shades and again proclaimed a gay indifference—
"Gracious! she *is* exclusive!" Winterbourne wondered
if she were seriously wounded and for a moment almost
wished her sense of injury might be such as to make it
becoming in him to reassure and comfort her. He had
a pleasant sense that she would be all accessible to a
respectful tenderness at that moment. He felt quite
ready to sacrifice his aunt—conversationally; to acknowledge she was a proud rude woman and to make
the point that they needn't mind her. But before he had
time to commit himself to this questionable mixture of
gallantry and impiety, the young lady, resuming her
walk, gave an exclamation in quite another tone. "Well,
here's mother! I guess she *hasn't* got Randolph to go to
bed." The figure of a lady appeared, at a distance, very
indistinct in the darkness; it advanced with a slow and
wavering step and then suddenly seemed to pause.

"Are you sure it's your mother? Can you make her
out in this thick dusk?" Winterbourne asked.

"Well," the girl laughed, "I guess I know my own
mother! And when she has got on my shawl too. She's
always wearing my things."

The lady in question, ceasing now to approach,
hovered vaguely about the spot at which she had
checked her steps.

"I'm afraid your mother doesn't see you," said Winterbourne. "Or perhaps," he added—thinking, with Miss
Miller, the joke permissible—"perhaps she feels guilty
about your shawl."

"Oh it's a fearful old thing!" his companion placidly
answered. "I told her she could wear it if she didn't
mind looking like a fright. She won't come here because
she sees you."

"Ah then," said Winterbourne, "I had better leave
you."

"Oh no—come on!" the girl insisted.

"I'm afraid your mother doesn't approve of my walk-ing with you."

She gave him, he thought, [the oddest]28 glance. "It isn't for me; it's for you—that is it's for *her*. Well, I don't know who it's for! But mother doesn't like any of my gentlemen friends. She's right down timid. She al-ways makes a fuss if I introduce a gentleman. But I *do* introduce them—almost always. If I didn't introduce my gentlemen friends to mother," Miss Miller added, in her small flat monotone, "I shouldn't think I was natural."

"Well, to introduce me," Winterbourne remarked, "you must know my name." And he proceeded to pro-nounce it.

"Oh my—I can't say all that!" cried his companion, much amused. But by this time they had come up to Mrs. Miller, who, as they drew near, walked to the parapet of the garden and leaned on it, looking intently at the lake and presenting her back to them. "Mother!" said the girl in a tone of decision—upon which the elder lady turned round. "Mr. Frederick Forsyth Winter-bourne," said the latter's young friend, repeating his lesson of a moment before and introducing him very frankly and prettily. "Common" she might be, as Mrs. Costello had pronounced her; [yet what provision was made by that epithet for her queer little native grace?29]

Her mother was a small spare light person, with a wandering eye, a scarce perceptible nose, and, as to make up for it, an unmistakeable forehead, decorated—but too far back, as Winterbourne mentally described it—with thin much-frizzled hair. Like her daughter Mrs. Miller was dressed with extreme elegance; she had enormous diamonds in her ears. So far as the young man could observe, she gave him no greeting—she cer-tainly wasn't looking at him. Daisy was near her, pulling

28 a serious
29 yet it was a wonder to Winterbourne that, with her com-monness, she had a singularly delicate grace.

her shawl straight. "What are you doing, poking round here?" this young lady enquired—yet by no means with the harshness of accent her choice of words might have implied.

"Well, I don't know"—and the new-comer turned to the lake again.

"I shouldn't think you'd want that shawl!" Daisy familiarly proceeded.

"Well—I do!" her mother answered [with a sound that partook for Winterbourne of an odd strain between mirth and woe.]30

"Did you get Randolph to go to bed?" Daisy asked.

"No, I couldn't induce him" [—and Mrs. Miller seemed to confess to the same mild fatalism as her daughter.]31 "He wants to talk to the waiter. He *likes* to talk to that waiter."

"I was just telling Mr. Winterbourne," the girl went on; and to the young man's ear her tone might have indicated that she had been uttering his name all her life.

"Oh yes!" he concurred—"I've the pleasure of knowing your son."

Randolph's mamma was silent; she kept her attention on the lake. But at last a sigh broke from her. "Well, I don't see how he lives!"

"Anyhow, it isn't so bad as it was at Dover," Daisy at least opined.

"And what occurred at Dover?" Winterbourne desired to know.

"He wouldn't go to bed at all. I guess he sat up all night—in the public parlour. He wasn't in bed at twelve o'clock: it seemed as if he couldn't budge."

"It was half-past twelve when I gave up," Mrs. Miller recorded with passionless accuracy.

It was of great interest to Winterbourne. "Does he sleep much during the day?"

30 with a little laugh.
31 said Mrs. Miller, very gently.

"I guess he doesn't sleep *very* much," Daisy rejoined.

"I wish he just *would!*" said her mother. "It seems as if he *must* make it up somehow."

"Well, I guess it's we that make it up. I think he's real tiresome," Daisy pursued.

After which, for some moments, there was silence. "Well, Daisy Miller," the elder lady then unexpectedly broke out, "I shouldn't think you'd want to talk against your own brother!"

"Well, he *is* tiresome, mother," said the girl, but with no sharpness of insistence.

"Well, he's only nine," Mrs. Miller lucidly urged.

"Well, he wouldn't go up to that castle, anyway," her daughter replied as for accommodation. "I'm going up there with Mr. Winterbourne."

To this announcement, very placidly made, Daisy's parent offered no response. Winterbourne took for granted on this that she opposed such a course; but he said to himself at the same time that she was a simple easily-managed person and that a few deferential protestations would modify her attitude. "Yes," he therefore interposed, "your daughter had kindly allowed me the honour of being her guide."

Mrs. Miller's wandering eyes attached themselves with an appealing air to her other companion, who, however, strolled a few steps further, gently humming to herself. "I presume you'll go in the cars," she then quite colourlessly remarked.

"Yes, or in the boat," said Winterbourne.

"Well, of course I don't know," Mrs. Miller returned. "I've never been up to that castle."

"It is a pity you shouldn't go," he observed, beginning to feel reassured as to her opposition. And yet he was quite prepared to find that as a matter of course she meant to accompany her daughter.

It was on this view accordingly that light was projected for him. "We've been thinking ever so much about going, but it seems as if we couldn't. Of course Daisy—she wants to go round everywhere. But there's a lady here—I don't know her name—she says she shouldn't think we'd want to go to see castles *here;* she should think we'd want to wait till we got t' Italy. It seems as if there would be so many there," continued Mrs. Miller with an air of increasing confidence. "Of course we only want to see the principal ones. We visited several in England," she presently added.

"Ah yes, in England there are beautiful castles," said Winterbourne. "But Chillon here is very well worth seeing."

"Well, if Daisy feels up to it—" said Mrs. Miller in a tone [that seemed to break under the burden of such conceptions.][32] "It seems as if there's nothing she won't undertake."

"Oh! I'm pretty sure she'll enjoy it!" Winterbourne declared. And he desired more and more to make it a certainty that he was to have the privilege of a *tête-à-tête* with the young lady who was still strolling along in front of them and softly vocalising. "You're not disposed, madam," he enquired, ["to make the so interesting excursion yourself?"][33]

So addressed Daisy's mother looked at him an instant with a certain scared obliquity and then walked forward in silence. Then, "I guess she had better go alone," she said simply.

It gave him occasion to note that this was a very different type of maternity from that of the vigilant matrons who massed themselves in the forefront of social intercourse in the dark old city at the other end of the lake. But his meditations were interrupted by hearing his name very distinctly pronounced by Mrs. Miller's unprotected daughter. "Mr. Winterbourne!" she piped from a considerable distance.

"Mademoiselle!" said the young man.

"Don't you want to take me out in a boat?"

[32] impregnated with a sense of the magnitude of the enterprise.

[33] "to undertake it yourself?"

"At present?" he asked.

"Why of course!" she gaily returned.

"Well, Annie Miller!" exclaimed her mother.

"I beg you, madam, to let her go," he hereupon eagerly pleaded; so instantly had he been struck with the romantic side of this chance to guide through the summer starlight a skiff freighted with a fresh and beautiful young girl.

"I shouldn't think she'd want to," said her mother. "I should think she'd rather go indoors."

"I'm sure Mr. Winterbourne wants to *take* me," Daisy declared. "He's so awfully devoted!"

"I'll row you over to Chillon under the stars."

"I don't believe it!" Daisy laughed.

"Well!" the elder lady again gasped, as in rebuke of this freedom.

"You haven't spoken to me for half an hour," her daughter went on.

"I've been having some very pleasant conversation with your mother," Winterbourne replied.

"Oh pshaw! I want you to take me out in a boat!" Daisy went on as if nothing else had been said. They had all stopped and she had turned round and was looking at her friend. Her face wore a charming smile, her pretty eyes gleamed in the darkness, she swung her great fan about. No, he felt, it was impossible to be prettier than that.

"There are half a dozen boats moored at that landing-place," and he pointed to a range of steps that descended from the garden to the lake. "If you'll do me the honour to accept my arm we'll go and select one of them."

She stood there smiling; she threw back her head; she laughed as for the drollery of this. "I like a gentleman to be formal!"

"I assure you it's a formal offer."

"I was bound I'd make you say something," Daisy agreeably mocked.

"You see it's not very difficult," said Winterbourne. "But I'm afraid you're chaffing me."

"I think not, sir," Mrs. Miller shyly pleaded.

"Do then let me give you a row," he persisted to Daisy.

"It's quite lovely, the way you say that!" she cried in reward.

"It will be still more lovely to do it."

"Yes, it would be lovely!" But she made no movement to accompany him; [she only remained an elegant image of free light irony.]³⁴

["I guess you'd better]³⁵ find out what time it is," her mother impartially contributed.

"It's eleven o'clock, madam," said a voice with a foreign accent out of the neighbouring darkness; and Winterbourne, turning, recognised the florid personage he had already seen in attendance. He had apparently just approached.

"Oh Eugenio," said Daisy, "I'm going out with Mr. Winterbourne in a boat!"

Eugenio bowed. "At this hour of the night, mademoiselle?"

"I'm going with Mr. Winterbourne," she repeated with her shining smile. "I'm going this very minute."

"Do tell her she can't, Eugenio," Mrs. Miller said to the courier.

"I think you had better not go out in a boat, mademoiselle," the man declared.

Winterbourne wished to goodness this pretty girl were not on such familiar terms with her courier; but he said nothing, and she meanwhile added to his ground. "I suppose you don't think it's proper! My!" she wailed; "Eugenio doesn't think anything's proper."

"I'm nevertheless quite at your service," Winterbourne hastened to remark.

³⁴ she only stood there laughing.
³⁵ "I should think you had better

"Does mademoiselle propose to go alone?" Eugenio asked of Mrs. Miller.

"Oh no, with this gentleman!" cried Daisy's mamma for reassurance.

"I *meant* alone with the gentleman." The courier looked for a moment at Winterbourne—the latter [seemed to make out in his face a vague presumptuous intelligence as at the expense of their companions][36]—and then solemnly and with a bow, "As mademoiselle pleases!" he said.

But Daisy broke off at this. "Oh I hoped you'd make a fuss! I don't care to go now."

"Ah but I myself shall make a fuss if you don't go," Winterbourne declared with spirit.

"That's all I want—a little fuss!" With which she began to laugh again.

"Mr. Randolph has retired for the night!" [the courier hereupon importantly announced.][37]

"Oh Daisy, now we can go then!" cried Mrs. Miller.

Her daughter turned away from their friend, [all lighted with her odd perversity.][38] "Good-night—I hope you're disappointed or disgusted or something!"

He looked at her gravely, taking her by the hand she offered. "I'm puzzled, if you want to know!" he answered.

"Well, I hope it won't keep you awake!" she said very smartly; and, under the escort of the privileged Eugenio, the two ladies passed toward the house.

Winterbourne's eyes followed them; he was indeed quite mystified. He lingered beside the lake a quarter of an hour, [baffled by the question][39] of the girl's sudden familiarities and caprices. But the only very definite conclusion he came to was that he should enjoy deucedly "going off" with her somewhere.

36 thought he was smiling
37 the courier announced, frigidly.
38 looking at him, smiling and fanning herself.
39 turning over the mystery

Two days later he went off with her to the Castle of Chillon. He waited for her in the large hall of the hotel, where the couriers, the servants, the foreign tourists were lounging about and staring. It wasn't the place he would have chosen for a tryst, but she had placidly appointed it. She came tripping downstairs, buttoning her long gloves, squeezing her folded parasol against her pretty figure, dressed exactly in the way that consorted best, to his fancy, with their adventure. He was a man of imagination and, as our ancestors used to say, of sensibility; as he took in her charming air and caught from the great staircase her impatient confiding step the note of some small sweet strain of romance, not intense but clear and sweet, seemed to sound for their start. [He could have believed he was *really* going "off" with her.][40] He led her out through all the idle people assembled—they all looked at her straight and hard: she had begun to chatter as soon as she joined him. His preference had been that they should be conveyed to Chillon in a carriage, but she expressed a lively wish to go in the little steamer[41]—there would be such a lovely breeze upon the water and they should see such lots of people. The sail wasn't long, but Winterbourne's companion found time for many characteristic remarks and other demonstrations, not a few of which were, from the extremity of their candour, slightly disconcerting. To the young man himself their small excursion showed so for delightfully irregular and incongruously intimate that, even allowing for her habitual sense of freedom, he had some expectation of seeing her appear to find in it the same savour. But it must be confessed that he was in this particular rather disappointed. Miss Miller was highly animated, she was in the brightest spirits; but she was clearly not at all in a nervous flutter—as she should have been to match *his* tension; she avoided neither his eyes nor those of any one else; she neither

[40] He could have believed he was going to elope with her.
[41] she declared that she had a passion for steamboats.

coloured from an awkward consciousness when she
looked at him nor when she saw that people were looking at herself. People continued to look at her a great
deal, and Winterbourne could at least take pleasure in
his pretty companion's distinguished air. He had been
privately afraid she would talk loud, laugh overmuch,
and even perhaps desire to move extravagantly about
the boat. But he quite forgot his fears; he sat smiling
with his eyes on her face while, without stirring from
her place, she delivered herself of a great number of
original reflections. It was the most charming innocent
prattle he had ever heard, for, by his own experience
hitherto, when young persons were so ingenuous they
were less articulate and when they were so confident
were more sophisticated. If he had assented to the idea
that she was "common," at any rate, *was* she proving
so, after all, or was he simply getting used to her com-
monness? Her discourse was for the most part of what
immediately and superficially surrounded them, but
there were moments when it threw out a longer look or
took a sudden straight plunge.

"What on *earth* are you so solemn about?" she suddenly demanded, fixing her agreeable eyes on her
friend's.

"*Am* I solemn?" he asked. "I had an idea I was
grinning from ear to ear."

"You look as if you were taking me to a prayer-
meeting or a funeral. If that's a grin your ears are very
near together."

"Should you like me to dance a hornpipe on the
deck?"

"Pray do, and I'll carry round your hat. It will pay
the expense of our journey."

"I never was better pleased in my life," Winterbourne
returned.

She looked at him a moment, then let it renew her
amusement. "I like to make you say those things.
You're a queer mixture!"

In the castle, after they had landed, [nothing could exceed the light independence of her humour.]⁴² She tripped about the vaulted chambers, rustled her skirts in the corkscrew staircases, flirted back with a pretty little cry and a shudder from the edge of the oubliettes and turned a singularly well-shaped ear to everything Winterbourne told her about the place. But he saw she cared little for mediaeval history and that the grim ghosts of Chillon loomed but faintly before her. They had the good fortune to have been able to wander without other society than that of their guide; and Winterbourne arranged with this companion that they shouldn't be hurried—that they should linger and pause wherever they chose. He interpreted the bargain generously—Winterbourne on his side had been generous—and ended by leaving them quite to themselves. Miss Miller's observations were marked by no logical consistency; for anything she wanted to say she was sure to find a pretext. She found a great many, in the tortuous passages and rugged embrasures of the place, for asking her young man sudden questions about himself, his family, his previous history, his tastes, his habits, his designs, and for supplying information on corresponding points in her own situation. Of her own tastes, habits and designs the charming creature was prepared to give the most definite and indeed the most favourable account.

"Well, I hope you know enough!" she exclaimed after Winterbourne had sketched for her something of the story of the unhappy Bonnivard. "I never saw a man that knew so much!" The history of Bonnivard had evidently, as they say, gone into one ear and out of the other. But this easy erudition struck her none the less as wonderful, and she was soon quite sure she wished Winterbourne would travel with them and "go round" with them: they too in that case might learn something about something. "Don't you want to come

---

⁴² the subjective element decidedly prevailed.

and teach Randolph?" she asked; "I guess he'd improve with a gentleman teacher." Winterbourne was certain that nothing could possibly please him so much, but that he had unfortunately other occupations. "Other occupations? I don't believe a speck of it!" she protested. "What do you mean now? You're not in business." The young man allowed that he was not in business, but he had engagements which even within a day or two would necessitate his return to Geneva. "Oh bother!" she panted, "I don't believe it!" and she began to talk about something else. But a few moments later, when he was pointing out to her the interesting design of an antique fireplace, she broke out irrelevantly: "You don't mean to say you're going back to Geneva?"

"It is a melancholy fact that I shall have to report myself there to-morrow."

She met it with a vivacity that could only flatter him. "Well, Mr. Winterbourne, I think you're horrid!"

"Oh don't say such dreadful things!" he quite sincerely pleaded—"just at the last."

"The last?" the girl cried; "I call it the very first! I've half a mind to leave you here and go straight back to the hotel alone." And for the next ten minutes she did nothing but call him horrid. Poor Winterbourne was fairly bewildered; no young lady had as yet done him the honour to be so agitated by the mention of his personal plans. His companion, after this, ceased to pay any attention to the curiosities of Chillon or the beauties of the lake; she opened fire on the special charmer in Geneva whom she appeared to have instantly taken it for granted that he was hurrying back to see. How did Miss Daisy Miller know of that agent of his fate in Geneva? Winterbourne, who denied the existence of such a person, was quite unable to discover; and he was divided between amazement at the rapidity of her induction and amusement at the directness of her criticism. She struck him afresh, in all this, as an extraordinary mixture of innocence and crudity. "Does she never allow you more than three days at a time?" Miss Miller wished ironically to know. "Doesn't she give you a vacation in summer? there's no one so hard-worked but they can get leave to go off somewhere at this season. I suppose if you stay another day she'll come right after you in the boat. Do wait over till Friday and I'll go down to the landing to see her arrive!" He began at last even to feel he had been wrong to be disappointed in the temper in which his young lady had embarked. If he had missed the personal accent, the personal accent was now making its appearance. It sounded very distinctly, toward the end, in her telling him she'd stop "teasing" him if he'd promise her solemnly to come down to Rome that winter.

"That's not a difficult promise to make," he hastened to acknowledge. "My aunt has taken an apartment in Rome from January and has already asked me to come and see her."

"I don't want you to come for your aunt," said Daisy; "I want you just to come for me." And this was the only allusion he was ever to hear her make again to his invidious kinswoman. He promised her that at any rate he would certainly come, and after this she forbore from teasing. Winterbourne took a carriage and they drove back to Vevey in the dusk; the girl at his side, her animation a little spent, was now quite distractingly passive.

In the evening he mentioned to Mrs. Costello that he had spent the afternoon at Chillon with Miss Daisy Miller.

"The Americans—of the courier?" asked this lady.

"Ah happily the courier stayed at home."

"She went with you all alone?"

"All alone."

Mrs. Costello sniffed a little at her smelling-bottle. "And that," she exclaimed, 'is the little abomination you wanted me to know!"

III

WINTERBOURNE, who had returned to Geneva the day after his excursion to Chillon, went to Rome toward the end of January. His aunt had been established there a considerable time and he had received from her a couple of characteristic letters. "Those people you were so devoted to last summer at Vevey have turned up here, courier and all," she wrote. "They seem to have made several acquaintances, but the courier continues to be the most *intime*. The young lady, however, is also very intimate with various third-rate Italians, with whom she rackets about in a way that makes much talk. Bring me that pretty novel of Cherbuliez's—'Paule Méré'—and don't come later than the 23d."

Our friend would in the natural course of events, on arriving in Rome, have presently ascertained Mrs. Miller's address at the American banker's and gone to pay his compliments to Miss Daisy. "After what happened at Vevey I certainly think I may call upon them," he said to Mrs. Costello.

"If after what happens—at Vevey and everywhere—you desire to keep up the acquaintance, you're very welcome. Of course you're not squeamish—a man may know every one. Men are welcome to the privilege!"

"Pray what is it then that 'happens'—here for instance?" Winterbourne asked.

"Well, the girl tears about alone with her unmistakeably low foreigners. As to what happens further you must apply elsewhere for information. She has picked up half a dozen of the regular Roman fortune-hunters of the inferior sort and she takes them about to such houses as she may put *her* nose into. When she comes to a party—such a party as she can come to—she brings with her a gentleman with a good deal of manner and a wonderful moustache."

"And where's the mother?"

"I haven't the least idea. They're very dreadful people."

Winterbourne thought them over in these new lights. "They're very ignorant—very innocent only, and utterly uncivilised. Depend on it they're not 'bad.'"

"They're hopelessly vulgar," said Mrs. Costello. "Whether or no being hopelessly vulgar is being 'bad' is a question for the metaphysicians. They're bad enough to blush for, at any rate; and for this short life that's quite enough."

The news that his little friend the child of nature of the Swiss lakeside was now surrounded by half a dozen wonderful moustaches checked Winterbourne's impulse to go straightway to see her. He had perhaps not definitely flattered himself that he had made an ineffaceable impression upon her heart, but he was annoyed at hearing of a state of affairs so little in harmony with an image that had lately flitted in and out of his own meditations; the image of a very pretty girl looking out of an old Roman window and asking herself urgently when Mr. Winterbourne would arrive. If, however, he determined to wait a little before reminding this young lady of his claim to her faithful remembrance, he called with more promptitude on two or three other friends. One of these friends was an American lady who had spent several winters at Geneva, where she had placed her children at school. She was a very accomplished woman and she lived in Via Gregoriana. Winterbourne found her in a little crimson drawing-room on a third floor; the room was filled with southern sunshine. He hadn't been there ten minutes when the servant, appearing in the doorway, announced complacently "Madame Mila!" This announcement was presently followed by the entrance of little Randolph Miller, who stopped in the middle of the room and stood staring at Winterbourne. An instant later his pretty sister crossed the threshold; and then, after a considerable interval, the parent of the pair slowly advanced.

["I guess I know you!"]⁴³ Randolph broke ground without delay.

"I'm sure you know a great many things"—and his old friend clutched him all interestedly by the arm. "How's your education coming on?"

Daisy was engaged in some pretty babble with her hostess, but when she heard Winterbourne's voice she quickly turned her head with a "Well, I declare!" which he met smiling. "I told you I should come, you know."

"Well, I didn't believe it," she answered.

"I'm much obliged to you for that," laughed the young man.

"You might have come to see me then," Daisy went on as if they had parted the week before.

"I arrived only yesterday."

"I don't believe any such thing!" the girl declared afresh.

Winterbourne turned with a protesting smile to her mother, but this lady evaded his glance and, seating herself, fixed her eyes on her son. "We've got a bigger place than this," Randolph hereupon broke out. "It's all gold on the walls."

Mrs. Miller, more of a fatalist apparently than ever, turned uneasily in her chair. "I told you if I was to bring you you'd say something!" she stated as for the benefit of such of the company as might hear it.

"I told *you!*" Randolph retorted. "I tell *you,* sir!" he added jocosely, giving Winterbourne a thump on the knee. "It *is* bigger too!"

As Daisy's conversation with her hostess still occupied her Winterbourne judged it becoming to address a few words to her mother—such as "I hope you've been well since we parted at Vevey."

Mrs. Miller now certainly looked at him—at his chin. "Not very well, sir," she answered.

⁴³ "I know you!"

"She's got the dyspepsia," said Randolph. "I've got it too. Father's got it bad. But I've got it worst!"

This proclamation, instead of embarrassing Mrs. Miller, seemed to soothe her by reconstituting the environment to which she was most accustomed. "I suffer from the liver," she amiably whined to Winterbourne. "I think it's this climate; it's less bracing than Schenectady, especially in the winter season. I don't know whether you know we reside at Schenectady. I was saying to Daisy that I certainly hadn't found any one like Dr. Davis and I didn't believe I *would*. Oh up in Schenectady, he stands first; they think everything of Dr. Davis. He has so much to do, and yet there was nothing he wouldn't do for *me*. He said he never saw anything like my dyspepsia, but he was bound to get at it. I'm sure there was nothing he wouldn't try, and I didn't care what he did to me if he only brought me relief. He was just going to try something new, and I just longed for it, when we came right off. Mr. Miller felt as if he wanted Daisy to see Europe for herself. But I couldn't help writing the other day that I supposed it was all right for Daisy, but that I didn't know as I *could* get on much longer without Dr. Davis. At Schenectady he stands at the very top; and there's a great deal of sickness there too. It affects my sleep."

Winterbourne had a good deal of pathological gossip with Dr. Davis's patient, during which Daisy chattered unremittingly to her own companion. The young man asked Mrs. Miller how she was pleased with Rome. "Well, I must say I'm disappointed," she confessed. "We had heard so much about it—I suppose we had heard too much. But we couldn't help that. We had been led to expect something different."

Winterbourne, however, abounded in reassurance. "Ah wait a little, and you'll grow very fond of it."

"I hate it worse and worse every day!" cried Randolph.

"You're like the infant Hannibal," his friend laughed.

"No I ain't—like any infant!" Randolph declared at a venture.

"Well, that's so—and you never *were!*" his mother concurred. "But we've seen places," she resumed, "that I'd put a long way ahead of Rome." And in reply to Winterbourne's interrogation, "There's Zürich—up there in the mountains," she instanced; "I think Zürich's real lovely, and we hadn't heard half so much about it."

"The best place we've seen's the *City of Richmond!*" said Randolph.

"He means the ship," Mrs. Miller explained. "We crossed in that ship. Randolph had a good time on the *City of Richmond.*"

"It's the best place [*I've* struck,"][44] the child repeated. "Only it was turned the wrong way."

"Well, we've got to turn the right way sometime," said Mrs. Miller [with strained but weak optimism.][45] Winterbourne expressed the hope that her daughter at least appreciated the so various interest of Rome, and she declared with some spirit that Daisy was quite carried away. "It's on account of the society—the society's splendid. She goes round everywhere; she has made a great number of acquaintances. Of course she goes round more than I do. I must say they've all been very sweet—they've taken her right in. And then she knows a great many gentlemen. Oh she thinks there's nothing like Rome. Of course it's a great deal pleasanter for a young lady if she knows plenty of gentlemen."

By this time Daisy had turned her attention again to Winterbourne, but in quite the same free form. "I've been telling Mrs. Walker how mean you were!"

"And what's the evidence you've offered?" he asked, a trifle disconcerted, for all his superior gallantry, by her inadequate measure of the zeal of an admirer who

---

[44] I've seen,"
[45] with a little laugh.

on his way down to Rome had stopped neither at
Bologna nor at Florence, simply because of a certain
sweet appeal to his fond fancy, not to say to his finest
curiosity. He remembered how a cynical compatriot
had once told him that American women—the pretty
ones, and this gave a largeness to the axiom—were at
once the most exacting in the world and the least en-
dowed with a sense of indebtedness.

"Why you were awfully mean up at Vevey," Daisy
said. "You wouldn't do most anything. You wouldn't
stay there when I asked you."

"Dearest young lady," cried Winterbourne, with generous passion, "have I come all the way to Rome only
to be riddled by your silver shafts?"

"Just hear him say that!"—and she gave an affec-
tionate twist to a bow on her hostess's dress. "Did you
ever hear anything so quaint?"

"So 'quaint,' my dear?" echoed Mrs. Walker more
critically—quite in the tone of a partisan of Winterbourne.

"Well, I don't know"—and the girl continued to
finger her ribbons. "Mrs. Walker, I want to tell you
something."

"Say, mother-r," broke in Randolph with his rough
ends to his words, "I tell you you've got to go. Eugenio'll raise something!"

"I'm not afraid of Eugenio," said Daisy with a toss
of her head. "Look here, Mrs. Walker," she went on,
"you know I'm coming to your party."

"I'm delighted to hear it."

"I've got a lovely dress."

"I'm very sure of that."

"But I want to ask a favour—permission to bring a
friend."

"I shall be happy to see any of your friends," said
Mrs. Walker, who turned with a smile to Mrs.
Miller.

"Oh they're not my friends," [cried that lady, squirm-

ing in shy repudiation. "It seems as if they didn't take
to *me*][46]—I never spoke to one of them!"

"It's an intimate friend of mine, Mr. Giovanelli,"
Daisy pursued without a tremor in her young clearness
or a shadow on her shining bloom.

Mrs. Walker had a pause and gave a rapid glance at
Winterbourne. "I shall be glad to see Mr. Giovanelli,"
she then returned.

"He's just the finest kind of Italian," Daisy pursued
with the prettiest serenity. "He's a great friend of mine
and the handsomest man in the world—except Mr.
Winterbourne! He knows plenty of Italians, but he
wants to know some Americans. It seems as if he was
crazy about Americans. He's tremendously bright. He's
perfectly lovely!"

It was settled that this paragon should be brought to
Mrs. Walker's party, and then Mrs. Miller prepared to
take her leave. "I guess we'll go right back to the
hotel," she remarked with a confessed failure of the
larger imagination.

"You may go back to the hotel, mother," Daisy
replied, "but I'm just going to walk round."

"She's going to go it with Mr. Giovanelli," Randolph
unscrupulously commented.

"I'm going to go it on the Pincio," Daisy peaceably
smiled, while the way that she "condoned" these things
almost melted Winterbourne's heart.

"Alone, my dear—at this hour?" Mrs. Walker asked.
The afternoon was drawing to a close—it was the hour
for the throng of carriages and of contemplative pedes-
trians. "I don't consider it's safe, Daisy," her hostess
firmly asserted.

"Neither do I then," Mrs. Miller thus borrowed
confidence to add. "You'll catch the fever as sure as
you live. Remember what Dr. Davis told you!"

[46] answered Daisy's mamma, smiling shyly, in her own
fashion.

["Give her some of that medicine before she starts in," Randolph suggested.]⁴⁷

The company had risen to its feet: Daisy, still showing her pretty teeth, bent over and kissed her hostess. "Mrs. Walker, you're too perfect," she simply said. "I'm not going alone; I'm going to meet a friend."

["Your friend won't keep you from catching the fever even if it *is* his own second nature," Mrs. Miller observed.]⁴⁸

["Is it Mr. Giovanelli that's the dangerous attraction?" Mrs. Walker asked without mercy.]⁴⁹

Winterbourne was watching the challenged girl; at this question his attention quickened. She stood there smiling and smoothing her bonnet-ribbons; she glanced at Winterbourne. Then, while she glanced and smiled, she brought out all affirmatively and without a shade of hesitation: "Mr. Giovanelli—the beautiful Giovanelli."

"My dear young friend"—and, taking her hand, Mrs. Walker turned to pleading—"don't prowl off to the Pincio at this hour to meet a beautiful Italian."

"Well, he speaks first-rate English," Mrs. Miller incoherently mentioned.

"Gracious me," Daisy piped up, "I don't want to do anything that's going to affect my health—or my character either! There's an easy way to settle it." Her eyes continued to play over Winterbourne. "The Pincio's only a hundred yards off, and if Mr. Winterbourne were as polite as he pretends he'd offer to walk right in with me!"

Winterbourne's politeness hastened to proclaim itself, and the girl gave him gracious leave to accompany her. They passed downstairs before her mother, and at the door he saw Mrs. Miller's carriage drawn up, with the

⁴⁷ "Give her some medicine before she goes," said Randolph.
⁴⁸ "Your friend won't keep you from getting the fever," Mrs. Miller observed.
⁴⁹ "Is it Mr. Giovanelli?" asked the hostess.

ornamental courier whose acquaintance he had made at Vevey seated within. "Good-bye, Eugenio," cried Daisy; "I'm going to take a walk!" The distance from Via Gregoriana to the beautiful garden at the other end of the Pincian Hill is in fact rapidly traversed. As the day was splendid, however, and the concourse of vehicles, walkers and loungers numerous, the young Americans found their progress much delayed. This fact was highly agreeable to Winterbourne, in spite of his consciousness of his singular situation. The slow-moving, idly-gazing Roman crowd bestowed much attention on the extremely pretty young woman of English race who passed through it, with some difficulty, on his arm; and he wondered what on earth had been in Daisy's mind when she proposed to exhibit herself unattended to its appreciation. His own mission, to her sense, was apparently to consign her to the hands of Mr. Giovanelli; but, at once annoyed and gratified, he resolved that he would do no such thing.

"Why haven't you been to see me?" she meanwhile asked. "You can't get out of that."

"I've had the honour of telling you that I've only just stepped out of the train."

"You must have stayed in the train a good while after it stopped!" she derisively cried. "I suppose you were asleep. You've had time to go to see Mrs. Walker."

"I knew Mrs. Walker——" Winterbourne began to explain.

"I know where you knew her. You knew her at Geneva. She told me so. Well, you knew me at Vevey. That's just as good. So you ought to have come." She asked him no other question than this; she began to prattle about her own affairs. "We've got splendid rooms at the hotel; Eugenio says they're the best rooms in Rome. We're going to stay all winter—if we don't die of the fever; and I guess we'll stay then! It's a great deal nicer than I thought; I thought it would be fearfully quiet—in fact I was sure it would be deadly pokey. I foresaw we would be going round all the time with one of those dreadful old men who explain about the pictures and things. But we only had about a week of that, and now I'm enjoying myself. I know ever so many people, and they're all so charming. The society's extremely select. There are all kinds—English and Germans and Italians. I think I like the English best. I like their style of conversation. But there are some lovely Americans. I never saw anything so hospitable. There's something or other every day. There's not much dancing —but I must say I never thought dancing was everything. I was always fond of conversation. I guess I'll have plenty at Mrs. Walker's—her rooms are so small."

When they had passed the gate of the Pincian Gardens Miss Miller began to wonder where Mr. Giovanelli might be. "We had better go straight to that place in front, where you look at the view."

Winterbourne at this took a stand. "I certainly shan't help you to find him."

"Then I shall find him without you," Daisy said with spirit.

"You certainly won't leave me!" he protested.

She burst into her familiar little laugh. "Are you afraid you'll get lost—or run over? But there's Giovanelli leaning against that tree. He's staring at the women in the carriages: did you ever see anything so cool?"

Winterbourne descried hereupon at some distance a little figure that stood with folded arms and nursing its cane. It had a handsome face, a hat artfully poised, a glass in one eye and a nosegay in its buttonhole. Daisy's friend looked at it a moment and then said: "Do you mean to speak to that thing?"

"Do I mean to speak to him? Why you don't suppose I mean to communicate by signs!"

"Pray understand then," the young man returned, "that I intend to remain with you."

Daisy stopped and looked at him without a sign of troubled consciousness, with nothing in her face but her charming eyes, her charming teeth and her happy dimples. "Well, she's a cool one!" he thought.

"I don't like the way you say that," she declared. "It's too imperious."

"I beg your pardon if I say it wrong. The main point's to give you an idea of my meaning."

The girl looked at him more gravely, but with eyes that were prettier than ever. "I've never allowed a gentleman to dictate to me or to interfere with anything I do."

"I think that's just where your mistake has come in," he retorted. "You should sometimes listen to a gentleman—the right one."

At this she began to laugh again. "I do nothing but listen to gentlemen! Tell me if Mr. Giovanelli is the right one."

The gentleman with the nosegay in his bosom had now made out our two friends and was approaching Miss Miller with obsequious rapidity. He bowed to Winterbourne as well as to the latter's compatriot; he seemed to shine, in his coxcombical way, with the desire to please and the fact of his own intelligent joy, though Winterbourne thought him not a bad-looking fellow. But he nevertheless said to Daisy: "No, he's not the right one."

She had clearly a natural turn for free introductions; she mentioned with the easiest grace the name of each of her companions to the other. She strolled forward with one of them on either hand; Mr. Giovanelli, who spoke English very cleverly—Winterbourne afterwards learned that he had practised the idiom upon a great many American heiresses—addressed her a great deal of very polite nonsense. He had the best possible manners, and the young American, who said nothing, reflected on that depth of Italian subtlety, so strangely opposed to Anglo-Saxon simplicity, which enables people to show a smoother surface in proportion as they're more acutely displeased. Giovanelli of course had counted upon something more intimate—

he had not bargained for a party of three; but he kept
his temper in a manner that suggested far-stretching
intentions. Winterbourne flattered himself he had
taken his measure. "He's anything but a gentleman,"
said the young American; "he isn't even a very plausible
imitation of one. He's a music-master or a penny-a-
liner or a third-rate artist. He's awfully on his good
behaviour, but damn his fine eyes!" [Mr. Giovanelli
had indeed great advantages; but it was deeply disgust-
ing to Daisy's other friend that something in her
shouldn't have instinctively discriminated against such
a type.][50] Giovanelli chattered and jested and made
himself agreeable according to his honest Roman lights.
It was true that if he was an imitation the imitation
was studied. "Nevertheless," Winterbourne said to himself, "a nice girl ought to know!" And then he came
back to the dreadful question of whether this *was* in fact
a nice girl. Would a nice girl—even allowing for her
being a little American flirt—make a rendezvous with
a presumably low-lived foreigner? The rendezvous in
this case indeed had been in broad daylight and in the
most crowded corner of Rome; but wasn't it possible
to regard the choice of these very circumstances as a
proof more of vulgarity than of anything else? Singular
though it may seem, Winterbourne was vexed that the
girl, in joining her *amoroso,* shouldn't appear more
impatient of his own company, and he was vexed pre-
cisely because of his inclination. It was impossible to
regard her as a wholly unspotted flower—she lacked
a certain indispensable fineness; and it would therefore
much simplify the situation to be able to treat her as
the subject of one of the visitations known to romanc-
ers as "lawless passions." That she should seem to
wish to get rid of him would have helped him to think

[50] Mr. Giovanelli had certainly a very pretty face; but Winterbourne felt a superior indignation at his own lovely fellow-
countrywoman's not knowing the difference between a spurious
gentleman and a real one.

more lightly of her, just as to be able to think more lightly of her would have made her less perplexing. Daisy at any rate continued on this occasion to present herself as an inscrutable combination of audacity and innocence.

She had been walking some quarter of an hour, attended by her two cavaliers and responding in a tone of very childish gaiety, as it after all struck one of them, to the pretty speeches of the other, when a carriage that had detached itself from the revolving train drew up beside the path. At the same moment Winterbourne noticed that his friend Mrs. Walker—the lady whose house he had lately left—was seated in the vehicle and was beckoning to him. Leaving Miss Miller's side, he hastened to obey her summons—and all to find her flushed, excited, scandalised. "It's really too dreadful"—she earnestly appealed to him. "That crazy girl mustn't do this sort of thing. She mustn't walk here with you two men. Fifty people have remarked her."

Winterbourne—suddenly and rather oddly rubbed the wrong way by this—raised his grave eyebrows. "I think it's a pity to make too much fuss about it."

"It's a pity to let the girl ruin herself!"

"She's very innocent," he reasoned in his own troubled interest.

"She's very reckless," cried Mrs. Walker, "and goodness knows how far—left to itself—it may go. Did you ever," she proceeded to enquire, "see anything so blatantly imbecile as the mother? After you had all left me just now I couldn't sit still for thinking of it. It seemed too pitiful not even to attempt to save them. I ordered the carriage and put on my bonnet and came here as quickly as possible. Thank heaven I've found you!"

"What do you propose to do with us?" Winterbourne uncomfortably smiled.

"To ask her to get in, to drive her about here for half an hour—so that the world may see she's not running absolutely wild—and then take her safely home."

"I don't think it's a very happy thought," he said after reflexion, "but you're at liberty to try."

Mrs. Walker accordingly tried. The young man went in pursuit of their young lady who had simply nodded and smiled, from her distance, at her recent patroness in the carriage and then had gone her way with her own companion. On learning, in the event, that Mrs. Walker had followed her, she retraced her steps, however, with a perfect good grace and with Mr. Giovanelli at her side. She professed herself "enchanted" to have a chance to present this gentleman to her good friend, and immediately achieved the introduction; declaring with it, and as if it were of as little importance, that she had never in her life seen anything so lovely as that lady's carriage-rug.

"I'm glad you admire it," said her poor pursuer, smiling sweetly. "Will you get in and let me put it over you?"

"Oh no, thank you!"—Daisy knew her mind. "I'll admire it ever so much more as I see you driving round with it."

"Do get in and drive round *with* me," Mrs. Walker pleaded.

"That would be charming, but it's so fascinating just as I am!"—with which the girl radiantly took in the gentlemen on either side of her.

"It may be fascinating, dear child, but it's not the custom here," urged the lady of the victoria, leaning forward in this vehicle with her hands devoutly clasped.

"Well, it ought to be then!" Daisy imperturbably laughed. "If I didn't walk I'd expire."

"You should walk with your mother, dear," cried Mrs. Walker with a loss of patience.

"With my mother dear?" the girl amusedly echoed. Winterbourne saw she scented interference. "My mother never walked ten steps in her life. And then, you know," she blandly added, "I'm more than five years old."

"You're old enough to be more reasonable. You're old enough, dear Miss Miller, to be talked about."

Daisy wondered to extravagance. "Talked about? What do you mean?"

"Come into my carriage and I'll tell you."

Daisy turned shining eyes again from one of the gentlemen beside her to the other. Mr. Giovanelli was bowing to and fro, rubbing down his gloves and laughing [irresponsibly;][51] Winterbourne thought the scene the most unpleasant possible. "I don't think I want to know what you mean," the girl presently said. "I don't think I should like it."

Winterbourne only wished Mrs. Walker would tuck up her carriage-rug and drive away; but this lady, as she afterwards told him, didn't feel she could "rest there." "Should you prefer being thought a very reckless girl?" she accordingly asked.

"Gracious me!" exclaimed Daisy. She looked again at Mr. Giovanelli, then she turned to her other companion. There was a small pink flush in her cheek; she was tremendously pretty. "Does Mr. Winterbourne think," she put to him with a wonderful bright intensity of appeal, "that—to save my reputation—I ought to get into the carriage?"

It really embarrassed him; for an instant he cast about—so strange was it to hear her speak that way of her "reputation." But he himself in fact had to speak in accordance with gallantry. The finest gallantry here was surely just to tell her the truth; and the truth, for our young man, as the few indications I have been able to give have made him known to the reader, was that his charming friend should listen to the voice of civilised society. He took in again her exquisite prettiness and then said the more distinctly: "I think you should get into the carriage."

[51] very agreeably;

Daisy gave the rein to her amusement. "I never heard anything so stiff! If this is improper, Mrs. Walker," she pursued, "then I'm *all* improper, and you had better give me right up. Good-bye; I hope you'll have a lovely ride!"—and with Mr. Giovanelli, who made a triumphantly obsequious salute, she turned away.

Mrs. Walker sat looking after her, and there were tears in Mrs. Walker's eyes. "Get in here, sir," she said to Winterbourne, indicating the place beside her. The young man answered that he felt bound to accompany Miss Miller; whereupon the lady of the victoria declared that if he refused her this favour she would never speak to him again. She was evidently wound up. He accordingly hastened to overtake Daisy and her more faithful ally, and, offering her his hand, told her that Mrs. Walker had made a stringent claim on his presence. He had expected her to answer with something rather free, something still more significant of the perversity from which the voice of society, though the lips of their distressed friend, had so earnestly endeavoured to dissuade her. But she only let her hand slip, as she scarce looked at him, through his slightly awkward grasp; while Mr. Giovanelli, to make it worse, bade him farewell with too emphatic a flourish of the hat.

Winterbourne was not in the best possible humour as he took his seat beside the author of his sacrifice. "That was not clever of you," he said candidly, as the vehicle mingled again with the throng of carriages.

"In such a case," his companion answered, ["I don't want to be clever—I only want to be *true!*"][52]

["Well, your truth has only offended the strange little creature—it has only put her off."][53]

"It has happened very well"—Mrs. Walker accepted

---

[52] "I don't wish to be clever, I wish to be *earnest!*"
[53] "Well, your earnestness has only offended her and put her off."

her work. "If she's so perfectly determined to compromise herself the sooner one knows it the better— one can act accordingly."

"I suspect she meant no great harm, you know," Winterbourne maturely opined.

"So I thought a month ago. But she has been going too far."

"What has she been doing?"

"Everything that's not done here. Flirting with any man she can pick up; sitting in corners with mysterious Italians; dancing all the evening with the same partners; receiving visits at eleven o'clock at night. Her mother melts away when the visitors come."

"But her brother," laughed Winterbourne, "sits up till two in the morning."

"He must be edified by what he sees. I'm told that at their hotel every one's talking about her and that a smile goes round among the servants when a gentleman comes and asks for Miss Miller."

"Ah we needn't mind the servants!" Winterbourne compassionately signified. "The poor girl's only fault," he presently added, "is her complete lack of education."

"She's naturally indelicate," Mrs. Walker, on her side, reasoned. "Take that example this morning. How long had you known her at Vevey?"

"A couple of days."

"Imagine then the taste of her making it a personal matter that you should have left the place!"

He agreed that taste wasn't the strong point of the Millers—after which he was silent for some moments; but only at last to add: "I suspect, Mrs. Walker, that you and I have lived too long at Geneva!" And he further noted that he should be glad to learn with what particular design she had made him enter her carriage.

"I wanted to enjoin on you the importance of your ceasing your relations with Miss Miller; that of your not appearing to flirt with her; that of your giving her no further opportunity to expose herself; that of your in short letting her alone."

"I'm afraid I can't do anything quite so enlightened as *that*," he returned. "I like her awfully, you know."

"All the more reason you shouldn't help her to make a scandal."

"Well, there shall be nothing scandalous in my attentions to her," he was willing to promise.

"There certainly will be in the way she takes them. But I've said what I had on my conscience," Mrs. Walker pursued. "If you wish to rejoin the young lady I'll put you down. Here, by the way, you have a chance."

The carriage was engaged in that part of the Pincian drive which overhangs the wall of Rome and overlooks the beautiful Villa Borghese. It is bordered by a large parapet, near which are several seats. One of these, at a distance, was occupied by a gentleman and a lady, toward whom Mrs. Walker gave a toss of her head. At the same moment these persons rose and walked to the parapet. Winterbourne had asked the coachman to stop; he now descended from the carriage. His companion looked at him a moment in silence and then, while he raised his hat, drove majestically away. He stood where he had alighted; he had turned his eyes toward Daisy and her cavalier. They evidently saw no one; they were too deeply occupied with each other. When they reached the low garden-wall they remained a little looking off at the great flat-topped pine-clusters of Villa Borghese; then the girl's attendant admirer seated himself familiarly on the broad ledge of the wall. The western sun in the opposite sky sent out a brilliant shaft through a couple of cloud-bars; whereupon the gallant Giovanelli took her parasol out of her hands and opened it. She came a little nearer and he held the parasol over her; then, still holding it, he let it so rest on her shoulder that both of their heads were hidden from Winterbourne. This young man stayed but a moment longer; then he began to walk.

But he walked—not toward the couple united beneath the parasol, rather toward the residence of his aunt Mrs. Costello.

IV

HE FLATTERED himself on the following day that there was no smiling among the servants when he at least asked for Mrs. Miller at her hotel. This lady and her daughter, however, were not at home; and on the next day after, repeating his visit, Winterbourne again was met by a denial. Mrs. Walker's party took place on the evening of the third day, and in spite of the final reserves that had marked his last interview with that social critic our young man was among the guests. Mrs. Walker was one of those pilgrims from the younger world who, while in contact with the elder, make a point, in their own phrase, of studying European society; and she had on this occasion collected several specimens of diversely-born humanity to serve, as might be, for textbooks. When Winterbourne arrived the little person he desired most to find wasn't there; but in a few moments he saw Mrs. Miller come in alone, very shyly and ruefully. This lady's hair, above the dead waste of her temples, was more frizzled than ever. As she approached their hostess Winterbourne also drew near.

"You see I've come all alone," said Daisy's unsupported parent. "I'm so frightened I don't know what to do; it's the first time I've ever been to a party alone—especially in this country. I wanted to bring Randolph or Eugenio or some one, but Daisy just pushed me off by myself. I ain't used to going round alone."

"And doesn't your daughter intend to favour us with her society?" Mrs. Walker impressively enquired.

"Well, Daisy's all dressed," Mrs. Miller testified with that accent of the dispassionate, if not of the philosophic, historian with which she always recorded the current incidents of her daughter's career. "She got dressed on purpose before dinner. But she has a friend of hers there; that gentleman—the handsomest of the Italians—that she wanted to bring. They've got going at the piano—it seems as if they couldn't leave off. Mr. Giovanelli does sing splendidly. But I guess they'll come before very long," Mrs. Miller hopefully concluded.

"I'm sorry she should come—[in that particular way,"][54] Mrs. Walker permitted herself to observe.

"Well, I told her there was no use in her getting dressed before dinner if she was going to wait three hours," returned Daisy's mamma. "I didn't see the use of her putting on such a dress as that to sit round with Mr. Giovanelli."

"This is most horrible!" said Mrs. Walker, turning away and addressing herself to Winterbourne. *"Elle s'affiche, la malheureuse.* It's her revenge for my having ventured to remonstrate with her. When she comes I shan't speak to her."

Daisy came after eleven o'clock, but she wasn't, on such an occasion, a young lady to wait to be spoken to. She rustled forward in radiant loveliness, smiling and chattering, carrying a large bouquet and attended by Mr. Giovanelli. Every one stopped talking and turned and looked at her while she floated up to Mrs. Walker. "I'm afraid you thought I never was coming, so I sent mother off to tell you. I wanted to make Mr. Giovanelli practise some things before he came; you know he sings beautifully, and I want you to ask him to sing. This is Mr. Giovanelli; you know I introduced him to you; he's got the most lovely voice and he knows the most charming set of songs. I made him go over them this evening on purpose; we had the greatest time at the hotel." Of all this Daisy delivered herself with the sweetest brightest loudest confidence, looking now at her hostess and now at all the room,

[54] in that way,"

while she gave a series of little pats, round her very white shoulders, to the edges of her dress. "Is there any one I know?" she as undiscourageably asked.

"I think every one knows you!" said Mrs. Walker as with a grand intention; and she gave a very cursory greeting to Mr. Giovanelli. This gentleman bore himself gallantly; he smiled and bowed and showed his white teeth, he curled his moustaches and rolled his eyes and performed all the proper functions of a handsome Italian at an evening party. He sang, very prettily, half a dozen songs, though Mrs. Walker afterwards declared that she had been quite unable to find out who asked him. It was apparently not Daisy who had set him in motion—this young lady being seated a distance from the piano and though she had publicly, as it were, professed herself his musical patroness or guarantor, giving herself to gay and audible discourse while he warbled.

"It's a pity these rooms are so small; we can't dance," she remarked to Winterbourne as if she had seen him five minutes before.

"I'm not sorry we can't dance," he candidly returned. "I'm incapable of a step."

"Of course you're incapable of a step," the girl assented. "I should think your legs *would* be stiff cooped in there so much of the time in that victoria."

"Well, they were very restless there three days ago," he amicably laughed; "all they really wanted was to dance attendance on you."

[55]"Oh my other friend—my friend in need—stuck to me; he seems more at one with his limbs than you are—I'll say that for him. But did you ever hear anything so cool," Daisy demanded, "as Mrs. Walker's wanting me to get into her carriage and drop poor Mr. Giovanelli, and under the pretext that it was proper? People have different ideas! It would have been

---

[55] "We paired off, that was much better," said Daisy.

most unkind; he had been talking about that walk for ten days."

"He shouldn't have talked about it at all," Winterbourne decided to make answer on this: "he would never have proposed to a young lady of this country to walk about the streets of Rome with him."

"About the streets?" she cried with her pretty stare. "Where then would he have proposed to her to walk? The Pincio ain't the streets either, I guess; and I besides, thank goodness, am not a young lady of this country. The young ladies of this country have a dreadfully pokey time of it, by what I can discover; I don't see why I should change my habits for [*such* stupids."][56]

"I'm afraid your habits are those of a ruthless flirt," said Winterbourne with studied severity.

"Of course they are!"—and she hoped, evidently, by the manner of it, to take his breath away. "I'm a fearful frightful flirt! Did you ever hear of a nice girl that wasn't? But I suppose you'll tell me now I'm not a nice girl."

He remained grave indeed under the shock of her cynical profession. "You're a very nice girl, but I wish you'd flirt with me, and me only."

"Ah thank you, thank you very much: you're the last man I should think of flirting with. As I've had the pleasure of informing you, you're too stiff."

"You say that too often," he resentfully remarked.

Daisy gave a delighted laugh. "If I could have the sweet hope of making you angry I'd say it again."

"Don't do that—when I'm angry I'm stiffer than ever. But if you won't flirt with me do cease at least to flirt with your friend at the piano. They don't," he declared as in full sympathy with "them," "understand that sort of thing here."

"I thought they understood nothing else!" Daisy cried with startling world-knowledge.

[56] *them."*

"Not in young unmarried women."

"It seems to me much more proper in young un-married[57] than in old married ones," she retorted.

"Well," said Winterbourne, "when you deal with natives you must go by the custom of the country. [American flirting is a purely American silliness; it has —in its ineptitude of innocence—no place in *this* system.][58] So when you show yourself in public with Mr. Giovanelli and without your mother—"

"Gracious, poor mother!"—and she made it beautifully unspeakable.

Winterbourne had a touched sense for this, but it didn't alter his attitude. "Though *you* may be flirting Mr. Giovanelli isn't—he means something else."

"He isn't preaching at any rate," [she returned.][59] "And if you want very much to know, we're neither of us flirting—not a little speck. We're too good friends for that. We're real intimate friends."

He was to continue to find her thus at moments inimitable. "Ah," he then judged, "if you're in love with each other it's another affair altogether!"

She had allowed him up to this point to speak so frankly that he had no thought of shocking her by the force of his logic; yet she now none the less immediately rose, blushing visibly and leaving him mentally to exclaim that the name of little American flirts was incoherence. "Mr. Giovanelli at least," she answered, sparing but a single small queer glance for it, a queerer small glance, he felt, than he had ever yet had from her—"Mr. Giovanelli never says to me such very disagreeable things."

It had an effect on him—he stood staring. The subject of their contention had finished singing; he left the piano, and his recognition of what—a little awkwardly —didn't take place in celebration of this might never-

[57] women
[58] Flirting is a purely American custom; it doesn't exist here.
[59] said Daisy with vivacity.

theless have been an acclaimed operatic tenor's series
of repeated ducks before the curtain. So he bowed
himself over to Daisy. "Won't you come to the other
room and have some tea?" he asked—offering Mrs.
Walker's slightly thin refreshment as he might have
done all the kingdoms of the earth.

Daisy at last turned [on Winterbourne a more natural and calculable light.][60] He was but the more
muddled by it, however, since so inconsequent a smile
made nothing clear—it seemed at the most to prove
in her a sweetness and softness that reverted instinctively to the pardon of offenses. "It has never occurred
to Mr. Winterbourne to offer me any tea," she said with
her finest little intention of torment and triumph.

"I've offered you excellent advice," the young man
permitted himself to growl.

"I prefer weak tea!" cried Daisy, and she went off
with the brilliant Giovanelli. She sat with him in the
adjoining room, in the embrasure of the window, for
the rest of the evening. There was an interesting per-
formance at the piano, but neither of these conversers
gave heed to it. When Daisy came to take leave of Mrs.
Walker this lady conscientiously repaired the weakness
of which she had been guilty at the moment of the girl's
arrival—she turned her back straight on Miss Miller
and left her to depart with what grace she might.
Winterbourne happened to be near the door; he saw
it all. Daisy turned very pale and looked at her mother,
but Mrs. Miller was humbly unconscious of any rup-
ture of any law or of any deviation from any custom.
She appeared indeed to have felt an incongruous impulse to draw attention to her own striking conformity.
"Good-night, Mrs. Walker," she said; "we've had a
beautiful evening. You see if I let Daisy come to
parties without me; I don't want her to go away without me." Daisy turned away, [looking with a small
white prettiness, a blighted grace,][61] at the circle near

[60] to Winterbourne, beginning to smile again.
[61] looking with a pale, grave face

the door: Winterbourne saw that for the first moment she was too much shocked and puzzled even for indignation. He on his side was greatly touched.

"That was very cruel," he promptly remarked to Mrs. Walker.

But this lady's face was also as a stone. "She never enters my drawing-room again."

Since Winterbourne then, hereupon, was not to meet her in Mrs. Walker's drawing-room he went as often as possible to Mrs. Miller's hotel. The ladies were rarely at home, but when he found them the devoted Giovanelli was always present. Very often the glossy little Roman, serene in success, but not unduly presumptuous, occupied with Daisy alone the florid salon enjoyed by Eugenio's care, Mrs. Miller being apparently ever of the opinion that discretion is the better part of solicitude. Winterbourne noted, at first with surprise, that Daisy on these occasions was neither embarrassed nor annoyed by his own entrance; but he presently began to feel that she had no more surprises for him [and that he really liked, after all, not making out what she was "up to."][62] She showed no displeasure for the interruption of her *tête-à-tete* with Giovanelli; she could chatter as freshly and freely with two gentlemen as with one, [and this easy flow had ever the same anomaly for her earlier friend that it was so free without availing itself of its freedom.][63] Winterbourne reflected that if she was seriously interested in the Italian it was odd she shouldn't take more trouble to preserve the sanctity of their interviews, and he liked her the better for her innocent-looking indifference and her inexhaustible gaiety. He could hardly have said why, but she struck him as a young person not formed for a troublesome jealousy. Smile at such a betrayal though the reader may, it was a fact

[62] the unexpected in her behaviour was the only thing to expect.

[63] there was always in her conversation the same odd mixture of audacity and puerility.

with regard to the women who had hitherto interested him that, given certain contingencies, Winterbourne could see himself afraid—literally afraid—of these ladies. It pleased him to believe that even were twenty other things different and Daisy should love him and he should know it and like it, he would still never be afraid of Daisy. It must be added that this conviction was not altogether flattering to her: [it represented that she was nothing every way if not light.][64]

But she was evidently very much interested in Giovanelli. She looked at him whenever he spoke; she was perpetually telling him to do this and to do that; she was constantly chaffing and abusing him. She appeared completely to have forgotten that her other friend had said anything to displease her at Mrs. Walker's entertainment. One Sunday afternoon, having gone to Saint Peter's with his aunt, Winterbourne became aware that the young woman held in horror by that lady was strolling about the great church under escort of her coxcomb of the Corso. It amused him, after a debate, to point out the exemplary pair—even at the cost, as it proved, of Mrs. Costello's saying when she had taken them in through her eye-glass: "That's what makes you so pensive in these days, eh?"

"I hadn't the least idea I was pensive," he pleaded.

"You're very much preoccupied; you're always thinking of something."

"And what is it," he asked, "that you accuse me of thinking of?"

"Of that young lady's, Miss Baker's, Miss Chandler's—what's her name?—Miss Miller's intrigue with that little barber's block."

"Do you call it an intrigue," he asked—"an affair that goes on with such peculiar publicity?"

"That's their folly," said Mrs. Costello, "it's not their merit."

[64] it was part of his conviction, or rather of his apprehension, that she would prove a very light young person.

"No," he insisted with a hint perhaps of the preoccupation to which his aunt had alluded—"I don't believe there's anything to be called an intrigue."

"Well"—and Mrs. Costello dropped her glass—"I've heard a dozen people speak of it: they say she's quite carried away by him."

"They're certainly as thick as thieves," our embarrassed young man allowed.

[Mrs. Costello came back to them, however, after a little; and Winterbourne recognised in this a further illustration—than that supplied by his own condition —of the spell projected by the case.][65] "He's certainly very handsome. One easily sees how it is. She thinks him the most elegant man in the world, the finest gentleman possible. She has never seen anything like him—he's better even than the courier. It was the courier probably who introduced him, and if he succeeds in marrying the young lady the courier will come in for a magnificent commission."

"I don't believe she thinks of marrying him," Winterbourne reasoned, "and I don't believe he hopes to marry her."

"You may be very sure she thinks of nothing at all. She romps on from day to day, from hour to hour, as they did in the Golden Age. I can imagine nothing more vulgar," said Mrs. Costello, whose figure of speech scarcely went on all fours. "And at the same time," she added, "depend upon it she may tell you any moment that she is 'engaged.' "

"I think that's more than Giovanelli really expects," said Winterbourne.

"And who is Giovanelli?"

["The shiny—but, to do him justice, not greasy—little Roman.][66] I've asked questions about him and learned something. He's apparently a perfectly respect-

---

[65] Mrs. Costello inspected the young couple again with her optical instrument.

[66] "The little Italian.

able little man. I believe he's in a small way a *cavaliere avvocato*. But he doesn't move in what are called the first circles. I think it really not absolutely impossible the courier introduced him. He's evidently immensely charmed with Miss Miller. If she thinks him the finest gentleman in the world, he, on his side, has never found himself in personal contact with such splendour, such opulence, such personal daintiness, as this young lady's. And then she must seem to him wonderfully pretty and interesting. Yes, he can't really hope to pull it off. That must appear to him too impossible a piece of luck. He has nothing but his handsome face to offer, and there's a substantial, a possibly explosive Mr. Miller in that mysterious land of dollars and six-shooters. Giovanelli's but too conscious that he hasn't a title to offer. If he were only a count or a *marchese!* What on earth can he make of the way they've taken him up?"

"He accounts for it by his handsome face and thinks Miss Miller a young lady *qui se passe ses fantaisies!*"

"It's very true," Winterbourne pursued, "that Daisy and her mamma haven't yet risen to that stage of—what shall I call it?—of culture, at which the idea of catching a count or a *marchese* begins. I believe them intellectually incapable of that conception."

"Ah but the *cavaliere avvocato* doesn't believe them!" cried Mrs. Costello.

Of the observation excited by Daisy's "intrigue" Winterbourne gathered that day at Saint Peter's sufficient evidence. A dozen of the American colonists in Rome came to talk with his relative, who sat on a small portable stool at the base of one of the great pilasters. The vesper-service was going forward in splendid chants and organ-tones in the adjacent choir, and meanwhile, between Mrs. Costello and her friends, much was said about poor little Miss Miller's going really "too far." Winterbourne was not pleased with what he heard; but when, coming out upon the great

steps of the church, he saw Daisy, who had emerged
before him, get into an open cab with her accomplice
and roll away through the cynical streets of Rome,
[the measure of her course struck him as simply there
to take.][67] He felt very sorry for her—not exactly that
he believed she had completely lost her wits, but because it was painful to see so much that was pretty and
undefended and natural sink so low in human estima-
tion. He made an attempt after this to give a hint to
Mrs. Miller. He met one day in the Corso a friend—
a tourist like himself—who had just come out of the
Doria Palace, where he had been walking through the
beautiful gallery. His friend "went on" for some moments about the great portrait of Innocent X, by
Velasquez, suspended in one of the cabinets of the
palace, and then said: "And in the same cabinet, by
the way, I enjoyed sight of an image of a different kind;
that little American who's so much more a work of
nature than of art and whom you pointed out to me last
week." In answer to Winterbourne's enquiries his friend
narrated that the little American—prettier now than
ever—was seated with a companion in the secluded
nook in which the papal presence is enshrined.

"All alone?" the young man heard himself disin-
genuously ask.

"Alone with a little Italian who sports in his buttonhole a stack of flowers. The girl's a charming beauty,
but I thought I understood from you the other day
that she's a young lady *du meilleur monde.*"

"So she is!" said Winterbourne; and having assured
himself that his informant had seen the interesting pair
but ten minutes before, he jumped into a cab and went
to call on Mrs. Miller. She was at home, but she
apologised for receiving him in Daisy's absence.

"She's gone out somewhere with Mr. Giovanelli.
She's always going round with Mr. Giovanelli."

[67] he could not deny to himself that she was going very far
indeed.

"I've noticed they're intimate indeed," Winterbourne concurred.

"Oh it seems as if they couldn't live without each other!" said Mrs. Miller. "Well, he's a real gentleman anyhow. I guess I have the joke on Daisy—that she *must* be engaged!"

"And how does your daughter *take* the joke?"

"Oh she just says she ain't. But she might as *well* be!" this philosophic parent resumed. "She goes on as if she was. But I've made Mr. Giovanelli promise to tell me if Daisy don't. I'd want to write to Mr. Miller about it—wouldn't you?"

Winterbourne replied that he certainly should; and the state of mind of Daisy's mamma struck him as so unprecedented in the annals of parental vigilance that [he recoiled before the attempt to educate at a single interview either her conscience or her wit.][68]

After this Daisy was never at home and he ceased to meet her at the houses of their common acquaintance, because, as he perceived, these shrewd people had quite made up their minds as to the length she must have gone. They ceased to invite her, intimating that they wished to make, and make strongly, for the benefit of observant Europeans, the point that though Miss Daisy Miller was a pretty American girl all right, her behaviour wasn't pretty at all—was in fact regarded by her compatriots as quite monstrous. Winterbourne wondered how she felt about all the cold shoulders that were turned upon her, and sometimes found himself suspecting with impatience that she simply didn't feel and didn't know. He set her down as hopelessly childish and shallow, as such mere giddiness and ignorance incarnate as was powerless either to heed or to suffer. Then at other moments he couldn't doubt that she carried about in her elegant and irresponsible little organism a defiant, passionate, perfectly observant

[68] gave up as utterly irrelevant the attempt to place her upon her guard.

consciousness of the impression she produced. He askcd himself whether the defiance would come from the consciousness of innocence or from her being essentially a young person of the reckless class. Then it had to be admitted, he felt, that holding fast to a belief in her "innocence" was more and more but a matter of gallantry too fine-spun for use. As I have already had occasion to relate, he was reduced without pleasure to this chopping of logic and vexed at his poor fallibility, his want of instinctive certitude as to how far her extravagance was generic and national and how far it was crudely personal. Whatever it was he had helplessly missed her, and now it was too late. She was "carried away" by Mr. Giovanelli.

A few days after his brief interview with her mother he came across her at that supreme seat of flowering desolation known as the Palace of the Caesars. The early Roman spring had filled the air with bloom and perfume, and the rugged surface of the Palatine was muffled with tender verdure. Daisy moved at her ease over the great mounds of ruin that are embanked with mossy marble and paved with monumental inscriptions. It seemed to him he had never known Rome so lovely as just then. He looked off at the enchanting harmony of line and colour that remotely encircles the city— he inhaled the softly humid odours and felt the freshness of the year and the antiquity of the place reaffirm themselves in deep interfusion. It struck him also that Daisy had never showed to the eye for so utterly charming; but this had been his conviction on every occasion of their meeting. Giovanelli was of course at her side, and Giovanelli too glowed as never before with something of the glory of his race.

"Well," she broke out upon the friend it would have been such mockery to designate as the latter's rival, "I should think you'd be quite lonesome!"

"Lonesome?" Winterbourne resignedly echoed.

"You're always going round by yourself. Can't you get any one to walk with you?"

"I'm not so fortunate," he answered, "as your gallant companion."

Giovanelli had from the first treated him with distinguished politeness; he listened with a deferential air to his remarks; he laughed punctiliously at his pleasantries; [he attached such importance as he could find terms for to Miss Miller's cold compatriot.][69] He carried himself in no degree like a jealous wooer; he had obviously a great deal of tact; he had no objection to any one's expecting a little humility of him. It even struck Winterbourne that he almost yearned at times for some private communication in the interest of his character for common sense; a chance to remark to him as another intelligent man that, bless him, *he* knew how extraordinary was their young lady and didn't flatter himself with confident—at least *too* confident and too delusive—hopes of matrimony and dollars. On this occasion he strolled away from his charming charge to pluck a sprig of almond-blossom which he carefully arranged in his buttonhole.

"I know why you say that," Daisy meanwhile observed. "Because you think I go round too much with *him!*" And she nodded at her discreet attendant.

"Every one thinks so—if you care to know," was all Winterbourne found to reply.

"Of course I care to know!"—she made this point with much expression. "But I don't believe a word of it. They're only pretending to be shocked. They don't really care a straw what I do. Besides, I don't go round so much."

"I think you'll find they do care. They'll show it—disagreeably," he took on himself to state.

[Daisy weighed the importance of that idea.][70] "How—disagreeably?"

[69] he seemed disposed to testify to his belief that Winterbourne was a superior young man.

[70] Daisy looked at him a moment.

"Haven't you noticed anything?" he compassionately asked.

"I've noticed *you*. [But I noticed you've no more 'give' than a ramrod the first time ever I saw you."

"You'll find at least that I've more 'give' than several others," he patiently smiled.][71]

"How shall I find it?"

"By going to see the others."

"What will they do to me?"

"They'll show you the cold shoulder. Do you know what that means?"

Daisy was looking at him intently; she began to colour. "Do you mean as Mrs. Walker did the other night?"

["Exactly as Mrs. Walker did the other night.][72]

She looked away at Giovanelli, still titivating with his almond-blossom. Then with her attention again on the important subject: "I shouldn't think you'd let people be so unkind!"

"How can I help it?"

"I should think you'd want to say something."

"I do want to say something"—and Winterbourne paused a moment. "I want to say that your mother tells me she believes you engaged."

"Well, I guess she does," said Daisy very simply.

The young man began to laugh. "And does Randolph believe it?"

"I guess Randolph doesn't believe anything." This testimony to Randolph's scepticism excited Winterbourne to further mirth, and he noticed that Giovanelli was coming back to them. Daisy, observing it as well, addressed herself again to her countryman. "Since you've mentioned it," she said, "I *am* engaged." He

[71] But I noticed you were as stiff as an umbrella the first time I saw you."

"You will find I am not so stiff as several others," said Winterbourne, smiling.

[72] "Exactly," said Winterbourne.

looked at her hard—he had stopped laughing. "You don't believe it!" she added.

He asked himself, and it was for a moment like testing a heart-beat; after which, "Yes, I believe it!" he said.

"Oh no, you don't," she answered. "But *if* you possibly do," she still more perversely pursued—"well, I ain't!"

Miss Miller and her constant guide were on their way to the gate of the enclosure, so that Winterbourne, who had but lately entered, presently took leave of them. A week later on he went to dine at a beautiful villa on the Caelian Hill, and, on arriving, dismissed his hired vehicle. The evening was perfect and he promised himself the satisfaction of walking home beneath the Arch of Constantine and past the vaguely-lighted monuments of the Forum. Above was a moon half-developed, whose radiance was not brilliant but veiled in a thin cloud-curtain that seemed to diffuse and equalise it. When on his return from the villa at eleven o'clock he approached the dusky circle of the Colosseum the sense of the romantic in him easily suggested that the interior, in such an atmosphere, would well repay a glance. He turned aside and walked to one of the empty arches, near which, as he observed, an open carriage—one of the little Roman street-cabs—was stationed. Then he passed in among the cavernous shadows of the great structure and emerged upon the clear and silent arena. The place had never seemed to him more impressive. One half of the gigantic circus was in deep shade while the other slept in the luminous dusk. As he stood there he began to murmur Byron's famous lines out of "Manfred"; but before he had finished his quotation he remembered that if nocturnal [meditation thereabouts was the fruit of a rich literary culture it was none the less deprecated by medical science. The air of other ages surrounded one; but the air of other ages, coldly analysed, was no better than a villainous miasma.][73] Winterbourne sought, however, toward the middle of the arena, a further reach of vision, intending the next moment a hasty retreat. The great cross in the centre was almost obscured; only as he drew near did he make it out distinctly. He thus also distinguished two persons stationed on the low steps that formed its base. One of these was a woman seated; her companion hovered before her.

Presently the sound of the woman's voice came to him distinctly in the warm night-air. "Well, he looks at us as one of the old lions or tigers may have looked at the Christian martyrs!" These words were winged with their accent, so that they fluttered and settled about him in the darkness like vague white doves. It was Miss Daisy Miller who had released them for flight.

"Let us hope he's not very hungry"—the bland Giovanelli fell in with her humour. "He'll have to take *me* first; you'll serve for dessert."

Winterbourne felt himself pulled up with final horror now—and, it must be added, with final relief. It was as if a sudden clearance had taken place in the ambiguity of the poor girl's appearances and the whole riddle of her contradictions had grown easy to read. [She was a young lady about the *shades* of whose perversity a foolish puzzled gentleman need no longer trouble his head or his heart.][74] That once questionable quantity *had* no shades—it was a mere black little blot. He stood there looking at her, looking at her companion too, and not reflecting that though he saw them vaguely he himself must have been more brightly presented. [He felt angry at all his shiftings of view—he felt

[73] meditations in the Colosseum are recommended by the poets, they are deprecated by the doctors. The historic atmosphere was there, certainly; but the historic atmosphere, scientifically considered, was no better than a villainous miasma.

[74] She was a young lady whom a gentleman need no longer be at pains to respect.

ashamed of all his tender little scruples and all his witless little mercies.][75] He was about to advance again, and then again checked himself; not from the fear of doing her injustice, but from a sense of the danger of showing undue exhilaration for this disburdenment of cautious criticism. He turned away toward the entrance of the place; but as he did so he heard Daisy speak again.

"Why it was Mr. Winterbourne! He saw me and he cuts me dead!"

What a clever little reprobate she was, he was amply able to reflect at this, and how smartly she feigned, how promptly she sought to play off on him, a surprised and injured innocence! But nothing would induce him to cut her either "dead" or to within any measurable distance even of the famous "inch" of her life. He came forward again and went toward the great cross. Daisy had got up and Giovanelli lifted his hat. Winterbourne had now begun to think simply of the madness, on the ground of exposure and infection, of a frail young creature's lounging away such hours in a nest of malaria. What if she *were* the most plausible of little reprobates? That was no reason for her dying of the *perniciosa*. "How long have you been 'fooling round' here?" he asked with conscious roughness.

Daisy, lovely in the sinister silver radiance, appraised him a moment, roughness and all. "Well, I guess all the evening." She answered with spirit and, he could see even then, with exaggeration. "I never saw anything so quaint."

"I'm afraid," he returned, "you'll not think a bad attack of Roman fever very quaint. This is the way people catch it. I wonder," he added to Giovanelli, "that you, a native Roman, should countenance such extraordinary rashness."

[75] He felt angry with himself that he had bothered so much about the right way of regarding Miss Daisy Miller.

"Ah," said this seasoned subject, "for myself I have no fear."

"Neither have I—for you!" Winterbourne retorted in French. "I'm speaking for this young lady."

Giovanelli raised his well-shaped eyebrows and showed his shining teeth, but took his critic's rebuke with docility. "I assured mademoiselle it was a grave indiscretion, but when was mademoiselle ever prudent?"

"I never was sick, and I don't mean to be!" mademoiselle declared. "I don't look like much, but I'm healthy! I was bound to see the Colosseum by moonlight—I wouldn't have wanted to go home without *that;* and we've had the most beautiful time, haven't we, Mr. Giovanelli? If there has been any danger Eugenio can give me some pills. Eugenio has got some splendid pills."

"*I* should advise you then," said Winterbourne, "to drive home as fast as possible and take one!"

Giovanelli smiled as for the striking happy thought. "What you say is very wise. I'll go and make sure the carriage is at hand." And he went forward rapidly.

Daisy followed with Winterbourne. He tried to deny himself the small fine anguish of looking at her, but his eyes themselves refused to spare him, and she seemed moreover not in the least embarrassed. He spoke no word; Daisy chattered over the beauty of the place: "Well, I *have* seen the Colosseum by moonlight—that's one thing I can rave about!" [Then noticing her companion's silence she asked him why he was so stiff—it had always been her great word. He made no answer, but he felt his laugh an immense negation of stiffness.][76] They passed under one of the dark archways; Giovanelli was in front with the carriage. Here Daisy stopped a moment, looking at her compatriot. "*Did* you believe I was engaged the other day?"

[76] Then, noticing Winterbourne's silence, she asked him why he didn't speak. He made no answer; he only began to laugh.

"It doesn't matter now what I believed the other day!" [he replied with infinite point.][77]

It was a wonder how she didn't wince for it. "Well, what do you believe now?"

"I believe it makes very little difference whether you're engaged or not!"

[He felt her lighted eyes fairly penetrate the thick gloom of the vaulted passage—as if to seek some access to him she hadn't yet compassed.][78] But Giovanelli, with a graceful inconsequence, was at present all for retreat. "Quick, quick; if we get in by midnight we're quite safe!"

Daisy took her seat in the carriage and the fortunate Italian placed himself beside her. "Don't forget Eugenio's pills!" said Winterbourne as he lifted his hat.

"I don't care," she unexpectedly cried out for this, "whether I have Roman fever or not!" On which the cab-driver cracked his whip and they rolled across the desultory patches of antique pavement.

Winterbourne—to do him justice, as it were—mentioned to no one that he had encountered Miss Miller at midnight in the Colosseum with a gentleman; in spite of which deep discretion, however, the fact of the scandalous adventure was known a couple of days later, with a dozen vivid details, to every member of the little American circle, and was commented accordingly. Winterbourne judged thus that the people about the hotel had been thoroughly empowered to testify, and that after Daisy's return there would have been an exchange of jokes between the porter and the cab-driver. But the young man became aware at the same moment of how thoroughly it had ceased to ruffle him that the little American flirt should be "talked about" by low-minded menials. These sources of current criticism a

[77] said Winterbourne, still laughing.
[78] He felt the young girl's pretty eyes fixed upon him through the thick gloom of the archway; she was apparently going to answer.

day or two later abounded still further: the little American flirt was alarmingly ill and the doctors now in possession of the scene. Winterbourne, when the rumour came to him, immediately went to the hotel for more news. He found that two or three charitable friends had preceded him and that they were being entertained in Mrs. Miller's salon by the all-efficient Randolph.

"It's going round at night that way, you bet—that's what has made her so sick. She's always going round at night. I shouldn't think she'd want to—it's so plaguey dark over here. [You can't see anything over here without the moon's right up. In America they don't go round by the moon!"][79] Mrs. Miller meanwhile wholly surrendered to her genius for unapparent uses; her salon knew her less than ever, and she was presumably now at least giving her daughter the advantage of her society. It was clear that Daisy was dangerously ill.

Winterbourne constantly attended for news from the sick-room, which reached him, however, but with worrying indirectness, though he once had speech, for a moment, of the poor girl's physician and once saw Mrs. Miller, who, sharply alarmed, struck him as thereby more happily inspired than he could have conceived and indeed as the most noiseless and light-handed of nurses. She invoked a good deal the remote shade of Dr. Davis, but Winterbourne paid her the compliment of taking her after all for less monstrous a goose. To this indulgence indeed something she further said perhaps even more insidiously disposed him. "Daisy spoke of you the other day quite pleasantly. Half the time she doesn't know what she's saying, but that time I think she did. She gave me a message—she told me to tell you. She wanted you to know she never was engaged to that handsome Italian who was always round. I'm

[79] You can't see anything here at night, except when there's a moon. In America, there's always a moon!"

sure I'm very glad; Mr. Giovanelli hasn't been near us since she was taken ill. I thought he was so much of a gentleman, but I don't call that very polite! A lady told me he was afraid I hadn't approved of his being round with her so much evenings. Of course it ain't as if their evenings were as pleasant as ours—since *we* don't seem to feel that way about the poison. I guess I *don't* see the point now; but I suppose he knows I'm a lady and I'd scorn to raise a fuss. Anyway, she wants you to realise she ain't engaged. I don't know why she makes so much of it, but she said to me three times 'Mind you tell Mr. Winterbourne.' And then she told me to ask if you remembered the time you went up to that castle in Switzerland. But I said I wouldn't give any such messages as *that*. [Only if she ain't engaged I guess I'm glad to realise it too."][80]

But, as Winterbourne had originally judged, the truth on this question had small actual relevance. A week after this the poor girl died; it had been indeed a terrible case of the *perniciosa*. A grave was found for her in the little Protestant cemetery, by an angle of the wall of imperial Rome, beneath the cypresses and the thick spring-flowers. Winterbourne stood there beside it with a number of other mourners; a number larger than the scandal excited by the young lady's career might have made probable. Near him stood Giovanelli, who came nearer still before Winterbourne turned away. Giovanelli, in decorous mourning, showed but a whiter face; his buttonhole lacked its nosegay and he had visibly something urgent—and even to distress—to say, which he scarce knew how to "place." He decided at last to confide it with a pale convulsion to Winterbourne. "She was the most beautiful young lady I ever saw, and the most amiable." To which he added in a moment: "Also—naturally!—the most innocent."

Winterbourne sounded him with hard dry eyes, but presently repeated his words, "The most innocent?"

[80] Only if she is not engaged, I'm sure I'm glad to know it."

"The most innocent!"

[It came somehow so much too late that our friend could only glare at its having come at all.][81] "Why the devil," he asked, "did you take her to that fatal place?"

Giovanelli raised his neat shoulders and eyebrows to within suspicion of a shrug. "For myself I had no fear; and *she*—she did what she liked."

Winterbourne's eyes attached themselves to the ground. "She did what she liked!"

It determined on the part of poor Giovanelli a further pious, a further candid, confidence. "If she had lived I should have got nothing. She never would have married me."[82]

[It had been spoken as if to attest, in all sincerity, his disinterestedness, but Winterbourne scarce knew what welcome to give it. He said, however, with a grace inferior to his friend's: "I dare say not."

The latter was even by this not discouraged. "For a moment I hoped so. But no. I'm convinced."][83]

Winterbourne took it in; he stood staring at the raw protuberance among the April daisies. When he turned round again his fellow mourner had stepped back.

He almost immediately left Rome, but the following summer he again met his aunt Mrs. Costello at Vevey. Mrs. Costello extracted from the charming old hotel there a value that the Miller family hadn't mastered the secret of. In the interval Winterbourne had often thought of the most interesting member of the trio— of her mystifying manners and her queer adventure. One day he spoke of her to his aunt—said it was on his conscience he had done her injustice.

"I'm sure I don't know"—that lady showed caution. "How did your injustice affect her?"

"She sent me a message before her death which I

---

[81] Winterbourne felt sore and angry.
[82] I am sure.
[83] "She would never have married you?"
"For a moment I hoped so. But no. I am sure."

didn't understand at the time. But I've understood it since. She would have appreciated one's esteem."

["She took an odd way to gain it! But do you mean by what you say," Mrs. Costello asked, "that she would have reciprocated one's affection?"][84]

As he made no answer to this she after a little looked round at him—he hadn't been directly within sight; but the effect of that wasn't to make her repeat her question. He spoke, however, after a while. "You were right in that remark that you made last summer. I was booked to make a mistake. I've lived too long in foreign parts." And this time she herself said nothing.

Nevertheless he soon went back to live at Geneva, whence there continue to come the most contradictory accounts of his motives of sojourn: a report that he's "studying" hard—an intimation that he's much interested in a very clever foreign lady.

—1878, 1909.

---

[84] "Is that a modest way," asked Mrs. Costello, "of saying that she would have reciprocated one's affection?"